LIKE MOTHER, LIKE DAUGHTERS

By Phil Giunta

Firebringer Press
Baltimore, Maryland

Like Mother, Like Daughters

By Phil Giunta

Editing & Proofreading by Sandra Zier-Teitler and Paul Balzé

Cover and Book design by Ethan H. Wilson

Cover Art by Laura Inglis

ISBN: 978-1-948178-01-3

Published by Firebringer Press

For Lynn Murphy—your advice on psychics and mediums helped inspire the character of Miranda Lorensen beginning with Testing the Prisoner, through By Your Side, and into this book.

For Amanda Headlee—your old house in the haunted woods of Kempton, PA inspired the opening scenes of this story. My wife and I will never forget ghost hunting at your place that Halloween night years ago. Good times!

Praise for Firebringer Take Two

"A two-tale treat for fans of things that go bump in the night -- starting with an appetizer about a vampire gnawing on an ethical dilemma, seasoned with macabre wit; and then serving a multi-course, multi-generational entree of ghostly mystery. So sit down, if you dare, to a supernatural double helping, but be forewarned: If you tend to read home alone after twilight, do so at your peril."

- Howard Weinstein,
New York Times bestselling author of *Galloway's Gamble*

Praise for "Like Mother, Like Daughters"

"I absolutely loved it. It grabbed my attention right from the beginning and I just wanted to keep reading."
- Deb Lerch on Goodreads

"There was a big problem—IT ENDED! Just when I didn't think Phil Giunta could top his last book, he did. I am going to cross my fingers right now and hope and pray to sweet baby Jesus that Phil will continue with more stories of Miranda and/or Andrea. I can see a really strong series coming out with these two characters."
- Beryl Snyder on Goodreads

By Phil Giunta

Testing the Prisoner
By Your Side

Edited by Phil Giunta:

Somewhere in the Middle of Eternity
Elsewhere in the Middle of Eternity
Meanwhile in the Middle of Eternity (Coming 2019)

Andrea Lorensen considered giving a whole new meaning to the term "touchscreen"—with her fist.

Instead, she restrained herself to a sigh as the dashboard GPS announced for the third time that it was "recalculating." *Sure, get me this far then screw me over... bastard.* She knew it was just embarrassment and frustration getting the best of her, especially since she was now 20 minutes late. The fact that her mom was with her didn't help.

"Lost in the woods on a frigid February night. Not how I prefer to start a paranormal investigation." From the passenger seat, Miranda Lorensen glanced at her daughter. "Just saying."

"I can barely see the street signs, okay? It's pitch black out here." Andrea pulled her mother's SUV onto a dirt road and turned around. "We must have passed it."

"Again."

Andrea rolled her eyes. "Don't be a smart-ass."

"Takes one to raise one. I thought you knew how to get there."

Andrea turned left onto what qualified as the main road in this podunk town, probably because it was the only one that was paved. "I've only been to Wendy's place once for a Halloween party, and I had a hard time finding it then. Can't your psychic mojo give us some direction?"

Miranda nodded toward the GPS. "That's what he's for."

As if on cue, the British baritone voice spoke up cheerfully. "In point one mile, turn left onto Pine Swamp Road."

Miranda snickered. "Now that's a name that inspires confidence. Just take it slow and let's keep our eyes open." In unison, both women perked up and pointed ahead. "There!"

The tree line parted just enough to reveal a narrow gravel road.

"Turn left," the GPS instructed.

"Now you tell me." Andrea swung the vehicle hard.

Miranda gripped the door handle with one hand while pressing her other palm against the dashboard. "Jeez, girl, who taught you how to drive?"

"You did."

"It shows."

Ahead of them, the high beams bounced and shook as they illuminated a well-traveled path of dirt and stone bordered by patches of snow and dead grass. Beyond that, more impenetrable darkness.

"And Wendy lives all alone out here?"

"Her parents own this little one story ranch. It's a tiny place, two bedrooms, one bath. They use it as a summer getaway, but Wendy lives in it during the school year. It's haunted, or so she says."

"Right. She hears voices and her cats get spooked."

"More than that. She also sees lights in the woods behind the house, and not flashlights either. They're up high near the treetops. They just float around and then vanish. She's dealing with it, but I think she's freaked—"

"Slow down."

"Why?"

"Something's coming. I can feel it."

"Where?"

Following the curve in the road, Andrea turned the vehicle slightly to the right—and screamed as a pair of headlights suddenly flashed on directly ahead of them before swerving to the left. Andrea was momentarily blinded as she veered the SUV wildly to avoid a collision. Just as quickly, she straightened out the wheel, narrowly missing a cluster of pine trees. Finally, she stomped on the brake pedal, propelling both women toward the windshield. Andrea's seatbelt sank into her chest before her body snapped back into the seat. She turned to her mother. "You okay?"

"Fine." Miranda nodded, pushing disheveled blonde locks away from her face. She reached over and did the same for her daughter. "You?"

Andrea slapped the steering wheel. "Bastard!" She threw open the driver's side door and leapt out.

"I'll take that as a yes," Miranda muttered. She followed Andrea's gaze to the fading red glow of taillights. "They're already gone. Nothing you can do now."

Using the flashlight app on her phone, Andrea inspected all four sides of the vehicle before climbing back in. "No damage that I can see. Friggin' redneck was driving with his lights off!" She sighed and sat back in her seat. "Sorry about this."

"Not your fault. That was some quick thinking behind the wheel."

"I had a good teacher, remember?"

"Did you happen to see what kind of car it was?"

"I think it was a pickup. I caught a flash of silver." Andrea narrowed her eyes. "I wonder if that was Ross."

"Ross?"

"Wendy's boyfriend, or maybe ex-boyfriend by now—you never know with her. I only talked to him once, at the Halloween party, but he picked Wendy up from campus a few times. I remember he drove a silver Chevy truck." Andrea exhaled sharply and frowned. "Mom, are you sure you're fine?"

"Yeah, why?"

"You're twirling your hair. You only do that when you're nervous. I know, because I do it, too."

Miranda dropped her hand. "Like mother, like daughter."

"I think we're both a bit rattled. Let's just get there and have a good night of ghost hunting."

As Andrea turned the SUV back onto the gravel, Miranda put a gentle hand on her forearm. "I can't pin it down, but something's wrong. I'm getting that old familiar pressure behind my eyes."

"The tunnel vision, too?"

Miranda shook her head. "Not yet, but the feeling is oppressive. The driver of that truck was running from something. Whatever it is, it's expecting us and it isn't very happy."

Andrea's shoulders slumped. "Thanks, Mom. You're giving me my second scare of the night and we're not even there yet."

***

Wendy was waiting for them. She stood just outside the front door in a loose-fitting sweatshirt and jeans that hugged the curves of her full figure. The cuffs were tucked into thick plush boots that every young woman seemed to be wearing lately.. Miranda had never understood the appeal in them. The girl's fiery red hair spilled around her shoulders and chest from beneath a gray fleece cap complete with earflaps and tassels.

Even as Miranda and her daughter approached, Wendy didn't smile. Standing beneath the exterior light, she regarded them with a detached expression, her hazel eyes glazed and distant.

"Hey." Andrea threw her arms around Wendy and pulled her close, yet the other woman's posture remained rigid as she returned a tepid embrace.

Andrea pulled back. "Are you okay?"

"I have a skull-splitting headache after dealing with my ex. You just missed him."

"Only by a few inches. He damn near ran us off the road. Didn't even have his lights on until we almost collided head-on."

"Doesn't surprise me. We ended up in an argument. It was an ugly scene."

"If he was angry, that would explain his reckless driving," Miranda chimed in.

"Oh." Andrea stepped back and gestured to Miranda. "Wendy, this is my mom."

"Nice to meet you." The girl smiled wanly and extended a hand. It was gelid to the touch and, for a moment, the pain behind Miranda's eyes flared sharply. It subsided as soon as their hands parted.

"Sorry if this is a bad time."

Wendy's gaze snapped into focus as she looked from Miranda to Andrea. Wincing slightly, she raised a hand to her stomach. "No, you need to be here. Tonight of all nights, I need your help."

Miranda and her daughter exchanged puzzled glances.

"Uh, sure," Andrea said. "Has there been more activity lately?"

"You could say that." Wendy opened the door. "Come on in, I'll give you a tour, although there isn't much to see. This place is just one giant box."

The living room was a narrow rectangle that spanned the entire width of the house. An entertainment center and sofa took up the left side. Behind the sofa, a vase filled with tiger lilies sat atop a half wall that opened to a small kitchen. To the right, in front of a cluttered desk, one of Wendy's cats was curled up on an office chair watching the visitors as they entered. The other cat was likely hiding elsewhere in the house.

Andrea pointed to an acoustic guitar suspended upright in its stand beside a small brick fireplace. "Oh, cool. When did you get that?"

"My mom brought that with her the last time she visited. I played a lot in high school. Don't get as much time with it anymore, but I wanted to get back into it. Actually, since it's been here, it strums every so often by itself as if someone's lightly running a finger across the strings. It only happened a few times, but I can't explain it."

"I suggest we leave a digital voice recorder on the floor in front of it," Miranda said.

Wendy led them down a narrow hallway toward the back of the house. Silhouettes of the women reflected in the glass of the storm door that opened out to the backyard and woods beyond.

Just past the bathroom, Wendy stopped and waved to her right. "I occasionally hear voices in this bedroom, which is why I sleep in the other one. I can never make out what they're saying and when I go to the doorway to listen, they shut up."

"Sounds like another candidate for a voice recorder," Andrea said. "What about the activity outside? You mentioned seeing lights in the woods?"

The color vanished from Wendy's face as she turned to gaze toward the back door. When she spoke, her tone was pensive. "Yeah… there was activity out there earlier tonight, in fact."

Miranda could sense Wendy's mounting fear. Whatever awaited them, it was in the woods—and Wendy knew it.

Andrea stepped up beside her friend. "You okay? If you don't want to go outside, it's fine. My mom and I can—"

"No." Wendy lowered her head and massaged her temples. "It's just this damn headache, but I want to show you where I see the lights."

"Take your time," Miranda said in a soothing tone. "Is there something about the lights we should know?"

Wendy didn't answer right away. With a sigh, she leaned against the wall.

Miranda looked at her daughter. Andrea shrugged and shook her head. Apparently, Wendy was not normally so withdrawn. From what Andrea had told her on the way here, Wendy was known to be vivacious and cheerful. Recently, however, something had changed. Andrea didn't know what.

After a moment, Wendy raised her head. "This is going to sound crazy, but I think they show up specifically for me. That's just an impression I get because my parents and brother never see them when they stay here."

"You think they're trying to communicate with you?" Andrea asked.

"I'm not sure. Maybe you can help me figure that out tonight."

"What do they look like?"

"Small bluish orbs that hover above the trees. They never make a sound. Eventually, they fade away. It's comforting but eerie at the same time. You know this area is haunted for miles around. People have seen spirits of American Indians and Civil War soldiers. Twelve years ago, two hikers were murdered on the Appalachian Trail not far from here. Their souls are supposedly still roaming the woods. It's a very active area."

"I can feel it," Miranda said. The pressure behind her eyes returned, blurring the edges of her vision. "There's definitely something here."

Andrea pulled a small LED flashlight from her coat pocket. "Let's go then."

Miranda held up a hand. "Hold on. Before we explore the woods, I want to get a few things from the car." She nodded toward the spare bedroom. "Andrea, can you please leave your voice recorder in here? I'd like to put the mini DV in here, too. Wendy, would you mind if I set up my laptop on your desk?"

"No problem."

"I have a night vision camera we can take with us outside."

"Do you need help?" Andrea asked.

"No, I'm good. Just stay put. Don't venture out there until we're set up in here. We'll all go together, okay?"

***

Andrea waited until her mother was out of earshot. "Wendy, are you sure you're all right? You've been down for weeks and I'm really concerned."

Wendy turned her head slowly, her expression inscrutable. "We need to go out there *now*."

"You're starting to freak me out. Can we just—"

Wendy gripped her hand with surprising strength. Andrea drew in a sharp breath. "Your hand is freezing. Don't you think you should put a coat and gloves on first?"

Wendy moved toward the door, dragging Andrea behind her. "Wendy, what the hell? We should wait for my mom. She's psychic or a medium or whatever. If she thinks there's something wrong—"

"She's right," Wendy opened the door, "but it can't wait any longer."

Andrea glanced over her shoulder to the front door. "Fine," she relented. "How far into the woods are we going?"

"Not far at all. He didn't have much time. I told him you were coming."

Andrea frowned. "What are you talking about?"

Wendy said no more as she stepped outside and strode across the small yard. Andrea followed her and noticed several pieces of firewood scattered across the frozen ground. She brought her flashlight to bear on the scene and noticed a half-cord of wood stacked neatly in a rectangular rack against the fence. It was obvious that one side had been disturbed.

"What happened here?"

"I was gathering wood for the fire when he showed up. I dropped some pieces during our argument. Come on."

Wendy opened the gate and hurried into the thicket.

"What's the rush?"

"You'll see."

Andrea weaved and ducked her way around bare branches while ice-frosted snow crunched under foot.

Wendy needed no illumination to make her way. For a minute, Andrea lost sight of her until the path curved to the right. There, Wendy stood with her back to Andrea, peering up into the sky.

At the lights.

Andrea gasped. "No shit." Two bluish-white orbs hovered above their heads. They seemed to pass through the branches as they glided among the trees. "Oh my God, they're just like you described."

Wendy didn't respond immediately. She seemed to be mesmerized. "They're here for me."

"What?" Andrea pulled her phone from her coat pocket and aimed it at the orbs. She took several steps forward, tracking them as they began to move out of view. When she spoke again, it was in hushed tones. She was afraid of scaring them off. "Damn it, mom, get out here with that camera. My mom got this cool night vision camera for Christmas. This is our first ghost hunt of the year and we were hoping to test it—"

Andrea turned around. Wendy was gone.

She aimed her flashlight along the path behind her. "Wendy?"

***

Miranda sighed as she gazed down the empty hallway. She called out to Andrea and Wendy, but there was no response—which only meant one thing. "These kids have no damn patience."

Carefully pushing aside a haphazard stack of notepads and index cards, Miranda placed her laptop and mini-DV camera on Wendy's desk. She made her way toward the back door, hoping that the girls were merely waiting outside.

A distant, terrified shriek told her otherwise.

Miranda threw open the storm door and bolted across the yard. "Andrea!"

She stepped on something solid that rolled under her foot, sending her stumbling forward. Snow-patched earth rose up to meet her. Miranda yelped as her chest landed squarely on another piece of firewood. She pushed herself up just enough to slide it out from beneath her and push it away.

"Mom, where are you!"

"I'm here," Miranda croaked. Wincing against the pain, she rolled onto her side and wrapped her arms around her chest, forcing her breaths into a calm rhythm.

When she opened her eyes again, two people stood above her a few feet away. The closest was a tall, stocky man wearing a leather jacket and baseball cap. He turned away just as Miranda gazed up at him, making it impossible to see his face. The girl, however, was unmistakable.

Wendy.

She cradled a few pieces of firewood in her arms as she stared wide-eyed at the man who was shouting at her. He was young, judging by his voice.

"You're fucking with the wrong family, bitch! You better keep your goddamn mouth shut."

"I'm not talking to you about this." Wendy held up a hand as she sidestepped him and made her way toward the house. "Just get the fuck out of here, before I call the—"

"Lying whore!" In a blur of motion, the man grabbed her arm and jerked her backward toward him. He brought his other hand up to her chest and shoved her effortlessly into the rack of firewood, knocking several pieces to the ground.

Miranda reached out to the chain link fence and pulled herself to her knees, all concern for herself forgotten. No one turned to look at her. This was a vision of events that must have occurred shortly before Miranda and her daughter arrived.

Wendy cried out as she crumpled to the ground. The young man moved in and grabbed her by the hair. She picked up a hefty piece of firewood and swung, but he anticipated her. He caught it easily and yanked it from her grasp, then raised it above his head. "You're not calling anyone, bitch."

"Oh, God, no..." Miranda could only watch in disgust as he clubbed Wendy in the stomach. She groaned and doubled over, but that wasn't enough for him. He continued his assault, beating her in the back of the head even after she collapsed into the snow. He stopped only when her body began twitching.

Seconds later, that stopped too.

Still on her knees, Miranda leaned forward, holding onto the fence for support. She wanted to vomit.

The man tossed the firewood aside. It landed exactly where Miranda had tripped. Despite the pain in her chest, she forced herself to her feet and spoke through gritted teeth. "You son of a bitch."

He lifted Wendy over his shoulder and carried her out through the fence and into the woods. Miranda watched until they vanished into the darkness.

Wendy's words from earlier came back to her. *You need to be here. Tonight of all nights, I need your help.*

***

"Andrea!" After following what she hoped was the right path through the woods, Miranda spotted the boots first. She slid to a halt in the snow and traced her flashlight along the body. Wendy's face was obscured by her thick mane of saffron hair, made crimson by congealing blood.

Andrea knelt over her friend. She looked up at Miranda. Her mouth hung open in confusion and horror. Tears fell from her face. "Where the hell were you? I was calling for you!" Struggling to catch her breath, she held out her hands above Wendy's prone form. "She's…"

"Dead, I know."

As Andrea broke down into quiet sobs, Miranda moved beside her and took her into her arms. "Honey, I'm so sorry. I would've been here sooner, but when I stepped outside, I… I had a vision of what happened."

Her daughter pulled back. "Tell me."

Miranda wiped the tears from Andrea's face. "It can wait. We need to—"

"No, I want to know who did this!"

Miranda hesitated. "The guy driving that truck killed Wendy in her backyard and dumped her out here just before we showed up. Problem was, it was too dark to see his face."

Andrea fell silent as she began to tremble, eyes wide. Miranda could only watch helplessly as cruel realization seized her daughter. "That means we were talking to her *ghost* the entire time?"

"That would explain a lot, like why I felt such heightened stress and fear when we first arrived, and why Wendy was so cold to the touch."

"Oh, God."

Miranda remained silent as Andrea stood and turned away. She leaned against a tree until she regained her composure. "At first, I thought she just tripped and fell, but I would have heard that. Then I saw the blood on her head… and she wasn't moving and…" Andrea doubled over, gritting her teeth. "Damn it."

Finally, she stood and ran a sleeve across her eyes. "We saw the orbs. Wendy said they were there for her."

"It's possible. They could have been the souls of just about anybody who lost their lives in these woods. Maybe they were here to shepherd Wendy to the next life, I don't know." Miranda glanced at the sky, but saw only the stars. "I really wish you'd waited for me before venturing out here."

"You're going to start on me now? It's not like I expected *this* to happen."

"Exactly. You're not experienced with the paranormal, and even if you were, investigators should never go anywhere alone because you never know what to expect. You've heard me say that more than once when I bring new members onto my team. At minimum, we work in pairs."

"I can handle myself, and Wendy was with me… sort of."

Miranda held up a hand. "We'll talk about this later. Right now, we need to go inside, put the equipment back in the car, and call the cops."

Andrea shook her head. "I'm not leaving her."

"You don't have to. I'll go to the house and call from the landline. There's no cell signal out here."

"What are we going to tell them?"

"Well, they're not likely to believe that her ghost led you to her body. It's probably better to say that the house was wide open when we got here. We noticed the firewood in disarray and the back gate open so we went looking for her."

"And tell them about Ross."

"We'll tell them about the truck."

Mother and daughter shared another embrace before Miranda started back toward the house.

***

Andrea dropped to her knees and closed her eyes. "I'm so sorry we were late. Please forgive me. It was my fault we got lost. I'm sorry." After a silent prayer, she opened her eyes and reeled back as a bluish-white sphere, no larger than a child's fist, hovered over Wendy's body.

"Wendy?" Andrea slowly reached out, but before she could touch it, the orb floated skyward and eventually joined two others that materialized above the trees. After a few seconds, all three faded into the night.

***

Four hours later, Wendy's body had been removed and the property cordoned off with caution tape. In the backyard, the cops had found blood on a loose piece of firewood. It had been bagged as evidence. In the living room, Miranda sat with one arm firmly at her side and the other around her daughter. In keeping her hands away from her head, she hoped to stifle her hair-twirling habit in front of the sheriff as he reviewed their statements.

Of course, that didn't stop her from fingering a lock of Andrea's hair instead.

Finally, the sheriff nodded grimly and closed his notepad. "Well, thank you both for your help. We'll contact her family tonight. I'll be in touch if I have more questions."

"Absolutely." Miranda and her daughter rose from the sofa. "Whatever we can do, please let us know."

"Actually, sir," Andrea spoke up in a timorous voice. "Before we leave, would you mind if we feed her cats?"

"Unfortunately, ma'am, this is a crime scene now. I'm not supposed to let you touch anything," the sheriff tapped his notepad against his other hand, "but you ladies don't seem like killers to me. Just make it quick. I need to go talk to my deputy. I'll be back in a few minutes to escort you out and lock up."

***

In the kitchen, the women kept their voices low as they filled food and water bowls and cleaned litter pans.

"You didn't tell him about your vision in the backyard," Andrea said.

"That would only have complicated things. Besides, I didn't see the guy's face. We told the sheriff about the truck. They found the firewood. Let them do their jobs. I'm more concerned about you right now."

If you only knew… "I'll be all right. I just need time, and I think I owe you an apology."

Her mother frowned. "For what, sweetie?"

"All these years listening to your ghost stories, I never really knew whether to believe you or not."

"Oh, I know, and now that you've had your own experience, you're finally convinced that your mom isn't an embarrassing whack-job."

"Something like that."

"If the spirits know you can see them, more will come. Most will be like Wendy, innocent lost souls just looking for help."

"Most?"

The sheriff stepped through the front door.

"We'll talk more about it later."

"Do you think I'll see her again?" Andrea whispered.

As if in response, a single, gentle strum startled both women. They turned to look at the guitar in the far corner of the living room. Even the sheriff was startled.

"I think you just got your answer."

***

Several people milled about on the wrap-around porch of the funeral home as Miranda pulled into the parking lot.

In the passenger seat, Andrea glanced at the dashboard clock. "How ironic."

Her mother backed into one of the last available parking spaces. "What's that?"

"I couldn't get us to Wendy's house on time Saturday night, but we can show up ten minutes early for her viewing. If we'd been on time then, we wouldn't be here now."

Andrea opened the car door, but stopped as her mother put a gentle hand on her arm.

"You need to stop beating yourself up. Her killer is the one to blame."

"If I didn't get us lost—"

"People get lost every day. That doesn't make them murderers."

"We're lucky the sheriff agreed with that."

"After over an hour of questioning and retracing every step we made. Look, maybe you won't listen to me because, hey, I'm only your mom," she pointed toward the funeral home, "but I'll bet not one person in there is going to blame you. In fact, I predict her family will be grateful that you found Wendy when you did. Otherwise, she could have been out there for days."

Andrea checked her watch. It was time.

***

As they made their way alongside the funeral home, an elderly woman in a dark gray and maroon dress waved a cane at them from the edge of the parking lot.

"Hello," she called out as she approached. Beyond the hem of her dress, thick calves moved her broad form with great effort. Miranda and Andrea stopped to wait for her.

"You know her?" Miranda muttered.

"Nope."

The woman stepped up to them and adjusted horn-rimmed glasses. "Sorry," she smiled. "Old and slow. I'm Nadine, Wendy's great-aunt." She extended a gloved hand to both women in turn. "You must be Andrea."

"Uh, yes, and this is my mother, Miranda."

"I know. Heard all about you from Wendy. Figured it was you from her description. She thought the world of you, young lady. Must have been horrible finding her in the woods like that. If you hadn't, she could've been out there for days. The family appreciates all you've done."

Miranda gave Andrea a gentle "told you so" nudge with her elbow.

Nadine shook her head. "This is a terrible world sometimes." She pointed her cane toward the porch and the gathering crowd. "She sure was popular."

Andrea turned and noticed three of her classmates among the mourners.

"Life's too short to wait in lines." Nadine reached out and took Andrea's hand. "You two come with me."

Bodies parted without question as Nadine led them through.

"Drea."

Andrea looked up to see her friends standing together. They looked at her expectantly, but Nadine's grip was firm as she charged ahead. "I'll catch up with you."

Miranda leaned close. "'Drea?'"

"It's just a nickname."

"'Drea.'"

"Hey, your friends call you 'Randy.'"

Somewhere along the way, Nadine released Andrea's hand. She was nowhere to be seen, but Andrea thought little of it as her attention became riveted on the open casket just a few steps ahead.

A young couple moved aside. They were nothing more than a blur as Andrea slowed her gait. She ignored her mother's hands on her shoulders; paid little attention to the susurration of the mourners filing in behind her.

"We should sign in," her mother whispered.

Andrea didn't have the energy to respond. She had no interest in a goddamn guest book. Wendy was dead. A vibrant life had been extinguished. That's all that mattered.

After a few seconds, her mother's hands slipped away. "I'll take care of it."

Wendy had been dressed in a full-length blue skirt and white blouse. Her hair, perfectly brushed, flowed elegantly over her shoulders down to her chest where her hands lay folded, clutching a tiger lily. Wendy's body was surrounded with them, and two lavish bouquets flanked the casket at either end.

Andrea rubbed her eyes in a vain attempt to suppress tears that would not be stopped. *I know you probably don't blame me, but I need to see you again… please. I want to tell you in person that I'm sorry. I'm sorry we were late. I need you to know that, or I'll carry this pain for the rest of my life. I know it sounds selfish, but I don't think I'm strong enough for that. It's bad enough that I'm going to miss you. It hurts. Please don't leave me like this.*

"Drea?"

Andrea started as a tall young man appeared beside her. She gazed up at Wendy's older brother, Dwight. Hazel eyes, normally bright and alert, were now bloodshot and distant. "Glazed with grief," her mom would sometimes call it.

"Sorry, I didn't mean to scare you," he whispered. "Just wanted to make sure you were…" His eyes shifted to the casket then to the floor. He sighed and shook his head. "None of us are okay right now. I don't know if we ever will be."

Andrea reached up and placed her hands on broad shoulders that slumped under her touch. Dwight smiled wanly as Andrea gently pulled him forward into her arms.

"Thank you for finding her." Dwight nodded toward the throng lined up at the doors. "I hope you didn't have to wait long. If I'd known when you were coming, I would have brought you directly in. My parents want to thank you, too."

"No worries. Your Aunt Nadine brought us in."

Dwight frowned. "Nadine?"

"Short, glasses, walks with a cane."

Dwight led her over to a nearby easel that held a collage of photographs from Wendy's life. In one photo, she sat beside Aunt Nadine. "Her?"

"Yep."

"Uh, that's impossible. She's been dead for over a decade. Are you sure it was her?"

Andrea closed her eyes. "Oh God, this is really happening to me."

"What is?"

"Nothing, never mind."

"Okay, well, could I call you later in the week? I'd like to know exactly what happened at the shack, if you don't mind."

"The shack?"

"That's what our family calls the house where Wendy was staying. We heard the official version from the sheriff, but I want to hear it from you, if that's all right."

Andrea agreed before steeling herself to meet his parents.

***

"Hey, you asleep?"

Beneath the covers, Andrea turned onto her side and felt Wendy's supple arm slide across her bare waist, drawing her closer. Andrea opened her eyes and smiled at the wall of wild saffron obscuring Wendy's face. A few disheveled locks stirred with each warm breath. Andrea craned her neck forward and kissed the top of Wendy's ginger head. The woman moaned softly in response.

Andrea reached over and parted her hair. Wendy's forehead was damp, her skin clammy to the touch. Andrea frowned and drew back her hand, fingertips coated in blood.

"Oh my God. Wendy, wake up. You're bleeding."

In a blur of motion, Wendy was on top of her, pinning her shoulders to the bed. Eyes wide with fear, the woman's face was covered in blood. It dripped from her hair onto Andrea's shoulders and chest.

"I need your help, Drea. Now more than ever."

***

Andrea awoke with a gasp as her body jolted violently. Though the passenger seat was reclined, she sat bolt upright. Warm air from the vents swept across her face, irritating her wide eyes.

"Sorry, sweetie. This onramp is riddled with potholes. That one snuck up on me." Her mother reached over and softly patted her leg. "How are you holding up?"

"I just saw someone I care about lying in a coffin, and tomorrow I'm driving back for her funeral. How do you think?" Andrea straightened the back of her seat and rubbed her eyes. "I'm all right. How long was I out?"

"About forty-five minutes. We have another thirty to go so feel free to go back to sleep. Unless, of course, you don't mind helping me stay awake. Especially since I have another hour on the road after I drop you off."

Andrea nodded, still shaking off the dream. "Can I ask you a question?"

"You just did."

"No, I'm serious. At Wendy's house, you said most of the spirits that come to you are looking for help. I know that from hearing your stories over the years, but what about the exceptions? What do they typically want?"

When her mother didn't answer immediately, Andrea glanced at her. "Mom?" She was obviously reluctant to meet her daughter's gaze. With a clenched jaw, she kept her eyes fixed firmly on the road.

"Mom, we've never really talked about this kind of thing and I'd like to know."

"I never brought it up before because I didn't want to scare you or your brothers, but given the circumstances, the more you know the better. In rare cases, ghosts have been known to get what they want by taking control of people and forcing them to do something dangerous, maybe even risk their lives."

"You mean possession?"

Her mother hesitated. "Yes, but when you say that, everyone conjures up images of *demonic* possession. In the case of ghosts, the avenues of possession are extremely limited. The most common is when a medium channels a spirit, usually in a controlled situation. Another is when someone is in an emotionally weakened state. That vulnerability makes them an easy target."

"Oh, God, please don't say that." Andrea rocked her head back against the seat. She wrapped her arms around herself to suppress a shiver. "Have you ever seen that happen?"

"I took a case once in Lancaster, Pennsylvania where a vindictive ghost was possessing people and driving them to suicide."

"You never told me about that. When was this?"

"About five years ago, during that summer when you and your brothers were traveling through Europe with your dad."

Andrea shook her head. "No offense, Mom, but I don't want your ability. I don't think I can deal with it."

"See, this is exactly what I was afraid of twenty years ago."

"What do you mean?"

Her mother sighed and shook her head, apparently unwilling to continue.

"What were you afraid of twenty years ago?"

"Something I'd hoped would never come up, especially as you got older and never exhibited the ability. Before your dad and I got married, we discussed having kids. He was all for it. He really wanted to be a father. I was the reluctant one. In fact, I was adamantly against it, at first."

"Why?"

"I didn't want to pass along this… ability. The world we live in is dangerous enough. I didn't want my child to grow up in fear of being stalked, harassed, or possibly tormented by something from the other side, something I couldn't control. Your father would have thought I was being ridiculous. You know how he gets whenever I talk about anything paranormal."

"So you never told him."

"No. I just… caved and gave him what he wanted."

Andrea was speechless. As if losing Wendy wasn't enough to break her heart, this confession from her mother dealt the crushing blow. She thought of her younger brothers.   Did her mother feel pressured to have them, too?

"Are you saying you regret having us?"

"What?" Her mother looked over, eyes wide. "Oh, no, honey, no."

She pulled off onto the shoulder and parked before putting a gentle hand under Andrea's chin. "I'm sorry. That didn't come out right. Listen to me, please. I don't regret a single moment. I love you and your brothers more than anyone in the world. I couldn't imagine my life without you.

"Back then, I was young and immature. Even now at forty-two, there are still times when my ability scares the hell out of me. Imagine how I was at your age. Once the spirits start coming, they don't stop. Growing up like that… at times, it was terrifying. I didn't want that for my children."

"It's okay, mom. I get it."

Her mother leaned forward and kissed Andrea on her forehead. "I love you."

"I love you too, and really, I get it, because I'm scared out of my mind, too."

"You're a late bloomer." Miranda peered into the rearview mirror before pulling out onto the highway. "I started seeing ghosts when I was six."

"When your parents took you to the Salem Witch Museum?"

"Yep. My first experience actually wasn't so bad. Camille was her name. I thought she was a living, breathing girl when she spoke to me. She was very polite for someone locked in a pillory. I didn't have enough sense to be scared by the fact that she disappeared a minute later."

"I remember you told me the story."

"Speaking of Salem, NEPCon is this weekend. I'm leaving Thursday night."

Andrea's shoulders slumped. Six months ago, her mother had signed a contract to speak at the Northeast Paranormal Convention's fifth anniversary event. "I forgot about that. Salem's what, five hundred miles away?"

"If there's an emergency, your dad's only a few hours from campus, but if any more ghosts show up and you need guidance on how to deal with them, call me immediately. I don't care who they are or what they want, okay?"

***

Seated atop the desk in her dorm room at Gustafson University, Andrea watched through the picture window as the amber rays of sunset faded behind a cluster of buildings across campus. Three days had passed since Wendy's funeral. Her brother, Dwight, had left a voicemail for Andrea yesterday. He wanted to know exactly what happened at "the shack" on Saturday night. Andrea didn't want to leave him hanging, but could she bear to run through it all again? It had taken the entire day for her to work up the courage to call him back.

She began the conversation by recounting the events from that terrifying evening, beginning with her near collision with Ross's pickup. Andrea hesitated when she spoke of finding Wendy's body. Her voice quivered and tears began to flow. Dwight waited patiently. She was careful to mention nothing of her interaction with Wendy's spirit.

"Did you actually see Ross driving that truck?"

No sooner had Dwight asked about Ross than the temperature in the room plummeted. Andrea's breath became a wispy vapor before her eyes.

What the—"Um, no, it was dark. I told that to the police. Why?"

"You'll probably hear this from the cops soon enough, but Ross is missing. They found his truck parked off the side of the road near the shack the night you were there, but he's disappeared."

Andrea reached back to pull a blanket from her bed. It wouldn't budge.

Ross was sitting on it.

Andrea's heart slammed in her chest.

"You still there?" Dwight asked.

"Uh… yeah."

"They think he might be—"

"Dead."

"I was going to say on the run."

"Maybe both."

"What?"

"Never mind. Dwight, I need to go, but I'll call you soon."

"Okay, but I just wanted to warn you in case Ross tries to come after you. He might have heard that you were there that night."

"I'm sure of it."

***

"I didn't kill her."

From his unkempt brown hair and scraggly beard to the bacon neck t-shirt, ripped jeans, and mud-crusted Doc Martens, he wasn't exactly the most impressive specimen Wendy had ever been with. Even his ghost had the grunge look. It occurred to Andrea that his outward appearance might simply be a manifestation of how she remembered him. Something her mother once told her about how the living perceive spirits.

Andrea folded her arms across her chest and pressed her back against the picture window—failing miserably to appear casual as she waited for Ross to impart the details of his demise.

"I guess you wouldn't believe me if I just told you what happened."

Unable to conjure a response, Andrea merely stared at him. *Maybe guilt drove him to suicide after murdering Wendy and he just needs to get it off his chest before he can move on.*

"Are you sure you don't want this blanket?" he asked. "You're shivering."

Andrea simply shook her head, unwilling to go near him. Ross slid from the bed and gathered up the blanket. Her apprehension must have been obvious, for he remained at arm's length.

"I didn't come here to hurt you. I need your help." Ross held out the blanket. "Please."

Andrea kept her gaze fixed on him as she reached for the blanket. Her fingers curled into the soft fabric.

And the room dissolved.

***

They stood facing each other in the night. Wide-eyed, Andrea glanced up at Ross as he unfurled the blanket and draped it around her shoulders.

"Don't touch me." She twisted away, but accepted the blanket nevertheless. Ross raised his hands and stepped back.

Andrea took in her surroundings. They were in a driveway alongside an old two-story stone home. A silver pickup truck was parked directly behind her.

Correction—*the* silver pickup. The one that had run her off the road the night Wendy was killed.

To her right, the property was bordered by what would normally have been dense woods. At this time of year, however, naked branches revealed the feeble glow of a gibbous moon.

"Where are we?" Andrea whispered, then yelped as the driveway was suddenly bathed in a stark, blinding white. She winced at the floodlights mounted along the side of the house.

Apparently, Andrea wasn't the only one startled. At the sound of crunching leaves, she spun and crept toward the edge of the driveway. *Something's out there.* Her eyes scanned the trees to the edge of the light, yet all was still.

Probably just an animal…

She pulled the blanket tighter around herself, more for protection than warmth. She was not cold here, wherever here was. Curious now, she started toward the rear of the driveway for a closer look at the truck.

With squeaking hinges, the side door of the house opened and Ross stepped out. Ignoring Andrea, he made his way around the truck to the driver's side.

She frowned. When did he slip into the house? "Going somewhere?"

When he didn't respond, she started toward him—

"I'm back here."

—and halted in mid-stride. Across the driveway, Ross leaned casually against the house, hands in his jacket pockets.

Andrea looked from one to the other, struggling to wrap her mind around what her eyes were showing her. "What the hell's happening?"

The other Ross stood beside his truck, the driver's side door wide open. He rifled through a thin stack of papers, apparently oblivious to Andrea's presence.

"He can't hear or see you," the first Ross said. "And you might not want to stand there."

"Why not?"

His expression was forlorn as he shifted his gaze slightly to the left, just over her shoulder.

She heard the footsteps then, quick and heavy.

Closing fast.

Andrea whirled just as a tall, broad figure charged at her from the woods. The man was upon her instantly, knife blade glinting in his right hand. Shrugging off the blanket, she threw her arms up to shield herself—an action that proved completely unnecessary as the intruder passed right through her and continued on toward the truck.

By the time Andrea's mind processed what had just happened, Ross was lying on his side, clutching his throat. Blood seeped between his fingers. His attacker dropped to his knees, pinning Ross's legs. Ross writhed and squirmed under the man's bulk to no avail—the predator had crippled his prey. Moving in for the kill, the man leaned forward and stabbed Ross several times in rapid succession.

He opened his mouth to cry out, but managed no more than a strained gurgle. Blood trickled from his lips. Enervated by his wounds, his struggling steadily abated. Finally, Ross lay still, breathing in spasms.

The man froze and met his victim's pleading gaze. Andrea expected him to speak, to offer an explanation for his brutal attack. Instead, the killer merely plunged the blade into Ross's chest.

Andrea screamed. Unable to tear her gaze away, she watched as Ross's arm dropped to his side. His body convulsed briefly as his lungs surrendered their final breath with a sickening rattle.

She began trembling uncontrollably as the Ross who had brought her here to witness this horror, approached and stood by her side. Finally, the murderer wiped the blade on his victim's jacket and rose to his feet. Folding the knife, he slipped it into his pocket and retrieved his cell phone. He began tapping silently on the screen.

"This is what happened to you on the night that Wendy was killed?"

Ross nodded. "By the same guy."

"But why?" Andrea forced herself to look away from the grisly scene. Disgust and anger overcame fear. This bastard had beaten her friend to death and dumped her in the woods like garbage. "Who is he?"

"You'll see."

"Just fuckin' tell me!"

"I'm doing better than that. I'm showing you so you'll understand. Do you think this is easy for me? You try watching your own murder. I had a life, plans, a future. Now I got nothing. I realize we barely knew each other, so I don't expect you to care about me, but we both cared about Wendy. If you don't want to help me, at least help her."

Andrea clenched her jaw and took a deep breath. Finally, she nodded. "Sorry. I'm just freaked out trying to process all of this. I'm way out of my element here." Her voice cracked as tears streaked her face.

Ross looked past her. "Well, here comes a big piece to the puzzle."

Behind them, the rumble of tires over gravel grew steadily louder as a maroon sedan, its headlights off, trundled toward them.

Andrea backed away, but Ross reached out and placed a hand on her arm. "Don't worry. There's no chance of injury here. You're actually still sitting on the desk in your dorm room. This is just a vision. They can't see or hear you."

"Yeah, well, this is all new to me." Andrea inhaled sharply and braced herself as the vehicle's bumper passed through their legs. By the time the sedan rolled to a stop, the pair stood waist-deep in the center of its hood, staring down through the windshield.

I wonder how Mom ever got used to this.

As if that experience didn't already baffle her, she let her mouth hang open as the driver stepped out of the car, leaving the door wide open. Though it was dark, Andrea recognized the high-and-tight hair, the deep-set eyes, the stocky frame.

"Wait, I know him. That's Dirk Brighton!"

The young man glanced nervously toward the house as he reached into the back seat with gloved hands and removed a dark, rolled bundle. Walking softly over the stones, he made his way toward the rear of the driveway.

Meeting him halfway, the murderer stepped away from Ross's truck and into the light. Andrea felt her face flush with heat. "Lance Brighton… no shit!"

Ross nodded solemnly, but offered no answer to the question in her eyes, not to mention the others churning in her head.

Lance and his older brother Dirk were two of Gustafson University's star athletes, profiled last month by the university magazine in an article titled "Bright Boys." Since then, the label stuck, albeit sarcastically in some circles. Most of the article had focused on Lance's nomination for the Doak Walker award for best college running back. Although Andrea was anything but a sports fan, there was no avoiding the fact that the Brightons had become campus celebrities and were practically beyond reproach.

Yet on Saturday night, Dirk had been an accessory to a murder committed by his brother.

Holy shit. If their father knew about this…! One of the longest tenured and most respected members of Gustafson's faculty, Gene Brighton had been with the university for over two decades as a Professor of Political Science and Philosophy. During the summer, he had moved into his new role as Dean of Humanities. Everyone who took his classes had nothing but admiration for the old man.

He would be devastated to see this. Andrea shook her head as the brothers unrolled a mummy-style sleeping bag and laid it beside Ross. Together, they lifted his body at either end.

"Christ, how many times did you stab him?" Dirk whispered.

"I got carried away."

"Just get him in the bag and don't get any blood on yourself."

"There's some on the driveway," Lance said.

Dirk nodded toward the truck. "Grab his keys. Go in the house and find a bucket. Fill it with hot water and rinse off this area before you go. Don't leave fingerprints anywhere."

Andrea turned to Ross. "How did your parents not hear any of this?"

"My dad took off when I was a kid. Haven't seen him since. My mom works second shift so I was home alone."

A moment later, Dirk slowly pulled the zipper closed. "OK, get it in the truck. You know where to dump it."

"Yep." Lance lifted the body like a rag doll and carried it to the back of the truck.

Andrea hesitated, unable to find a delicate way to ask. "Where did he—?"

"You familiar with Devil's Pool?"

She shook her head. "I'm not from around here."

"It's part of Stewart Lake. If you tell the cops Devil's Pool, they'll know."

"They're going to ask me how I know."

Ross smiled thinly. "You'll think of something, but please be careful."

Andrea paused. "Look, it's not that I don't want to help, but I really am new at this. I might need to call someone for advice."

"Advice?"

"Well, you're only my second ghost."

***

"Girl, what the hell are you talking about?"

Andrea opened her eyes to find her roommate, Nicherra, staring back at her quizzically. "What?"

"You just said I was your second ghost."

Andrea's gaze fell on the blanket clutched in her hands. "No, uh, sorry. I had a bad dream."

"How can you fall asleep sitting against a window?" Nicherra waved dismissively. "Never mind, I don't want to know. Didn't you say you had some place to be tonight?"

Andrea looked at the alarm clock on her side of the desk. *Damn it!*

She had 15 minutes to get changed and haul it across campus to the student center for Wendy's memorial. A small room on the third floor had been made available to classmates who wanted to stop by and share their memories or simply commiserate.

Wincing at the twinge between her shoulder blades, Andrea slid from the desk and tossed the blanket onto her bed.

"So what are you doing tonight?" she asked, gathering dark blue pants and a white blouse from her closet.

"Probably going to the gym to shoot some hoops for a few hours. Hey, I'm sorry about your friend. Tell you what, if I found a body in the woods like that, they'd have heard me screaming ten miles away. In fact, they wouldn't have heard a damn thing, 'cause I wouldn't have been there looking for ghosts in the first place."

Andrea smiled wanly and nodded toward the bathroom. "I better get changed."

"What are you, shy?"

"Uh, well—"

"Girl, we've been roommates for a month now and you're still changing in the bathroom. We have the same parts; mine are just darker than yours, right? So what are you worried about? You think I'm going to hide every time I need to strip down? Hell, no. Besides, from what I can see, you got nothing to be ashamed of."

Andrea's face flushed again. "Well, I also want to freshen up first."

Nicherra shrugged. "Suit yourself."

***

After checking into her room at the Salem Waterfront Hotel, Miranda rolled her luggage into the corner before tossing her backpack—and herself—onto the bed. She closed her eyes for a few seconds before glancing at her watch. Damn! Her first discussion panel at NEPCon was scheduled to start within the hour. With a groan, she sat up and began rummaging through her backpack until she found her tablet.

As its title implied, "Early Encounters" required each panelist to recount his or her first contact with the paranormal. Fortunately, Miranda was prepared. Weeks before the convention, she had decided to be as entertaining as possible by describing her childhood experience in the form of a short story told in the third person. She opened the document on her tablet and read it through one final time…

***

Outside the Salem Witch Dungeon Museum, six-year-old Miranda Lorensen looked on as her dad and older brother stuck their heads and hands through the holes in the fake pillories. Sometimes, they were called stocks, but Miranda had learned the word pillory today and she thought it sounded funny. There was nothing funny about this museum, though. Seeing a bunch of dummies hanging by their necks had scared her. Miranda preferred her witches on broomsticks, like the plastic ones that her parents hung in the windows this time of year.

As her mom took pictures, Miranda couldn't help but giggle as her dad and brother made silly faces for the camera. A cold breeze rustled her hair and gathered nearby autumn leaves into an orange and gold whirlwind. Miranda stared at it in wonder. Her family didn't seem to notice at all.

Behind her, a soft voice called out, "Little girl?"

Miranda turned, eyes flashing wide at the sight of a slim-faced teenager, her head and hands in a pillory that had not been there a moment ago. This one didn't look fake like the others. It was made with real wood and the holes were smaller, tighter. There was no way for the girl to get out. She was locked in by metal brackets on either side. Her white bonnet looked just like the ones worn by some of the dummies in the museum, but hers was tilted and smudged with nearly as much dirt as her bruised face. Long dark blonde hair, soaking wet, was matted around her forehead. Some of it stuck to the wood on either side of her head.

"Where did you come from?" Miranda asked, staring into the girl's ice blue eyes.

"I might ask you the same question. I have been here for hours."

"Why?"

"They accuse me of witchcraft."

"What does that mean?"

The girl flipped her hands over, palms up. "I do not know. Whatever witches do. Devil worship, or so they tell me."

"You don't look like a witch."

"Well, I would thank you to know I am not."

"Then why are you in there?"

"They do not believe me. They say I talk to demons, but I swear to be a God-fearing woman. I say my prayers and attend church faithfully. The devil and I could not be farther apart."

"I don't understand."

"Never mind now. Do not worry your pretty little head over it. What is your name?"

"Miranda."

"Such an elegant name. I have never heard the like."

"What's yours?

"Camille. It means attendant at the altar, or so my mother told me. Might I ask you for a favor, Miranda?"

Miranda shrugged. "Sure."

"Could you please fetch me some water? I have had neither food nor drink since yesterday evening."

"Okay, I'll be right back. I need to ask my mom and then I'll get you water."

"Bless you, Miranda."

Miranda spun around to find her dad and brother still posing in the phony pillories. She walked over to her mother snapping pictures a few feet away.

"Mom, Camille needs water."

"What, honey?" Her mother looked down at her. "Who's Camille?"

Miranda pointed to thin air. Slowly, she lowered her arm as she glanced left and right. "She was just there."

Her dad and brother backed out of the pillories and made their way over. Dad crouched down and put his arm around her. "There's no one there, Randy Panda."

"She was."

"Maybe someone was playing a joke on you."

Miranda shook her head. "No. They thought she was a witch but I don't think she was."

"So you saw a possible witch named Camille. What did she look like?"

"She had blonde hair and blue eyes. Just like me."

"Oh, just like you? And what was she wearing?"

Miranda shrugged. "Just a bonnet."

"Just a bonnet?" her mom said. "She was a naked witch?"

Everyone laughed.

Miranda stomped her foot. "No! She didn't have a body, just a head and hands."

"But she wanted water."

Miranda nodded.

Her mom sighed as she took Miranda's hand and started toward the street. "Miranda Ruth Lorensen, you have one vivid imagination."

***

Onstage in the hotel ballroom, Miranda finished reading her story to enthusiastic applause. When the audience quieted down, she continued. "Since that time, I've communicated with nearly fifty spirits. You may think that's a low number, but most of the time, I get impressions or feelings more so than direct contact. When we're investigating a location, I sometimes experience visions of incidents that occurred in the past. Interaction with a spirit is less common, but it's always remarkable when it happens."

In the back of the ballroom, a runner entered and held up a cardboard STOP sign. The panel's moderator nodded in acknowledgement. "Well, I'm afraid that's all the time we have. I'd like to thank our panelists for an hour of engaging and chilling stories, and thank you out there in the audience for attending. We're here all weekend, folks."

After exchanging compliments with the moderator and fellow panelists, Miranda made her way backstage to find a familiar face waiting for her.

"Girl, you totally rock."

Miranda smiled as she opened her arms to embrace one of her oldest friends. "Stephanie! I was wondering where you were."

The founder of the Route I-95 Ghost Hunters, known as the "I-95ers" for short, Stephanie Fantini was also the guest relations representative for NEPCon. Although they were four states apart now, Stephanie had lived in Miranda's hometown of Baltimore, and for nearly ten years, the two had been as close as sisters. In fact, they were not only the same age, but shared the same birthday.

Physically, however, the two couldn't be more distinct. Red highlights in short, raven hair swept down along Stephanie's neck to frame an olive complexion. She was a few inches shorter than Miranda and had gained about 15 pounds since they'd last met. "Phantom" Fantini, as she was known in many circles, made no secret about her love of Italian food.

"Sorry, Randy, I meant to text you earlier, but I've been putting out little fires all day. My team and I are going to dinner after the con closes at seven. Care to join us?"

"I'd love to. Let me guess, Italian place?"

"Greek diner. I was outvoted. You feel up to a little investigating later tonight?"

"Absolutely, but I didn't bring any equipment."

"We have everything you need. After dinner, we're heading up to Wenham to check out the Abbott houses, two historic homes related to the Salem

Witch Trials. I think they might interest you since Ruth Abbott and her daughter, Camille, were hanged together on charges of witchcraft."

"Actually, Ruth Abbott was hanged for murder. I'm not sure why, but she killed her brother-in-law, Nathaniel, while Camille was in the pillory awaiting execution for witchcraft."

"Someone did their research."

"I'm a history teacher, how could I not?"

"Oh, Randy, you definitely have to come with us tonight. You might make another connection to Camille, or one of the other Abbotts."

"You're on."

***

Andrea mulled over the events of the past few months as she hurried across campus to Wendy's memorial.

Wendy and Lance Brighton had started dating in November, although, according to the rumor mill, he'd always had a roving eye for a few of the blondes on the cheerleading squad. Apparently, the rest of him had soon followed when he started seeing two of them over the holiday break. He hadn't been discreet about it, either. Wendy had learned about it via Twitter, triggering a shit-storm on social media among everyone in their circle.

Just days into the spring semester, Wendy and Lance had broken up after a brief but intense conversation in the middle of the cafeteria. Andrea hadn't been there, but she'd heard about it. Shortly after, Wendy had become severely withdrawn. Her usual blithe manner had eroded into an overwhelming anxiety bordering on fear. At the time, Andrea sensed there was something more, something deeper, than the ephemeral heartache of a jilted lover. Yet, despite her best efforts, Wendy had refused to open up.

Most of their friends had casually dismissed Wendy's sudden mood swing. "She'll get over it," they'd said. "You know Wendy. She always bounces back!"

Their words of consolation to Wendy had been shallow and cliché, nothing more than thinly veiled schadenfreude. Even now, most of them just wanted a chance with the jock.

They can have the bastard.

After her vision of Ross's murder, Andrea's mind whirled with questions. What had Wendy been hiding after her breakup with Lance? Why did he kill her and Ross? And why the hell was Dirk involved? Andrea realized that she'd been nervously twirling a lock of her hair. With a sigh, she dropped her hand from her shoulder. *I really need to break that habit. I'm turning into my Mom.*

Finally, she reached the student center and pushed aside her anxiety as she climbed the steps to the third floor. Though Wendy's death would haunt her for years to come, this was a night to honor her life.

Straightening the front of her blouse, Andrea made her way down the hall. Murmuring voices and the faint stench of burned coffee led her to a small lounge normally used by the student counseling staff. Plush chairs and small round tables were lined up around the perimeter. Approximately twenty of her friends and fellow students were milling about. She recognized most of them. As her eyes scanned the dimly lit room, she was disgusted at the sight of four women from her dorm gathered around Lance Brighton. They smiled and listened to him with rapt attention as he prattled on about his workout regimen.

Fucking murderer. You got balls showing up here. I'm going to find a way to bring you down, bright boy.

As if feeling her gaze searing into his skull, Lance looked directly at her. After a double take, he excused himself and approached.

Shit.

"Excuse me, is your name Andrea?"

"Yes."

"I thought so. I was hoping to meet you." Lance extended a hand and smiled thinly. "Lance Brighton."

Andrea maintained a glacial expression to mask her revulsion. Undaunted, she accepted the gesture with a firm grip. "Yes, I know. I've seen you in action."

Lance bowed his head humbly just as an arm slid across Andrea's shoulders. She recognized the red and yellow Superman symbol tattooed on the slender forearm even before the body leaned into her.

"How you holdin' up, Drea?" It was Penny, a junior business major and one of the few women in their circle who didn't swoon over the jocks, preferring geeky guys instead. Penny was well known as a party girl, but she had a keen mind for business and technology. Unfortunately, it was clouded with booze at the moment, judging by her demeanor—and her breath.

"I'm hanging in there."

Penny moved behind her and began massaging her shoulders. "You're really tense, honey."

Lance took a step closer. He towered over Andrea as he spoke in a low voice. "I hear you're the one that found Wendy's body."

After you killed her, you piece of—"Yeah."

"That must have been horrible."

"I'll never forget it."

"They said you saw Ross driving away from her house."

"I saw his truck. It ran me off the road. I don't know who was driving it."

Lance held her gaze. Andrea didn't flinch, despite the fluttering in her stomach and the hands gripping her shoulders. She felt like a boxer in the middle of the ring before the big fight, staring down her opponent. Or up in this case. Way up.

"Ross… fuckin' pussy," Penny interjected, breaking the awkward silence and slurring every other word. "If I ever see that fucker, I'll gouge his fuckin' eyes out. I'd love to know where he is right now… fucker."

If only you knew…

Penny slipped her hands from Andrea's shoulders and hugged her around the waist, resting her head against the nape of her neck. She'd taken Wendy's death harder than most and it showed. Penny began weeping, sending tremors through Andrea's neck and shoulders.

Andrea turned and gave Penny's arm a tender squeeze. "We should probably go sit down."

Lance checked his watch.

"I'm going to head out. I don't do well at these things."

"Is that why you weren't at her funeral?"

"I didn't think it'd be appropriate, after what happened between us."

Andrea clenched her jaw as she watched Lance hurry from the room. She envisioned herself bashing his head in with a baseball bat or, better still, a crowbar.

Penny rested her chin on Andrea's shoulder. "Time to talk about Wendy?"

"Yep."

"Can you help me to a chair?"

This is going to be a long night.

***

"Dad."

Gene Brighton looked up from his laptop to find his youngest son standing in the doorway of his office. He frowned. "Lance, are you all right? You look distressed."

Lance stepped into the office and closed the door. "I think we have a problem. I just came from Wendy's memorial."

"I told you to stay away from that."

"Just listen to me, please. I had a reason to go. That girl, Andrea Lorensen, was there."

"The one who found the body."

Lance nodded quickly. "I think she knows. I think she saw me driving Ross's truck."

"Lance, slow down. Take a seat."

"No, Dad. I talked to her. You know, fishing for information."

Brighton closed his eyes and took a deep breath. "You talked to her? What did you say?"

"Nothing incriminating."

"What… did… you… say?"

Lance repeated his exchange with Andrea. "The look in her eyes, the tone of her voice… it just felt like she knew something."

Brighton sat back in his chair and thought about yesterday's lunch conversation with the Director of Campus Security. He'd learned that some of the cameras mounted around campus were not yet activated. There were a few blind spots—areas not yet under surveillance—including the grounds outside the student center where Wendy's memorial was being held.

Lance leaned over the desk. "Dad, even if she didn't see me behind the wheel, what if she or the cops found something at Wendy's house that could incriminate me? Incriminate us?"

"We had a solid alibi when the police questioned us on Sunday," Brighton reminded him. "It's been nearly a week. They haven't bothered us since."

"The investigation isn't over. They're still looking for Wendy's killer. Right now, Ross is their top suspect, but if they find his body, do you think it'll take them long to put the pieces together?"

Brighton rose from his seat and stepped around his desk until he stood before Lance. He placed his hands on either side of his son's face. "When your mother lay dying, the cancer eating her brain, I promised her that I would do everything in my power to see you and your brother successful. Ten years ago, I promised her that I would mold our boys into men she would be proud of." "I've heard this before, Dad."

Brighton pressed his hands into Lance's face. "Well, here's something new. I'll be damned if that little whore and her redneck boyfriend are going to destroy everything I've built. Same goes for this Lorensen girl. Do you understand me?"

Lance nodded silently.

Brighton smiled. "Look at you now. Tall and strong, able to look me straight in the eye. Your mother would definitely be proud."

"How can you say that after what we did?"

"What we did was protect my investment, and my promise."

"After talking with this bitch a few minutes ago, I'm not so sure how protected we are."

Brighton held up a hand. "She has nothing on us. If she did, she would have gone to the police already. Still, she's a loose end that could present a problem if she keeps digging."

"What should we do?"

"Call your brother."

"Why?"

"We're going to take a walk over to the student center."

"You can't be serious."

"The security cameras on that end of campus aren't working yet, so if we want to determine exactly what she knows, why don't we just ask her?"

Brighton reached into the pocket of his coat hanging on the inside of his office door. He produced a switchblade and pressed the button. With a click, the blade flipped open.

"Politely, of course."

***

Thankfully, the lounge had been well stocked with tissues.

Andrea wiped her eyes yet again after listening to nearly two hours of touching—and mostly hilarious—memories shared by fellow students. Some of them had known Wendy since high school, but even those who had only met her during their time at Gustafson, like Andrea, had stories to share. Such had been Wendy's effect on those close to her.

Eventually, the group began to disperse. Some departed immediately, while others remained to socialize or console one another. Andrea turned to Penny and found her fast asleep in her chair. At least she didn't snore. Two of Penny's friends and dorm-mates made their way over. After a few wisecracks, they agreed to escort her safely back to her room. They'd obviously become accustomed to the chore.

On her way out, Andrea overheard snippets of conversations, some mentioning Ross, others Lance. The moment she emerged into the hallway, a cluster of people lowered their voices. They spoke in hushed tones and flashed perfunctory smiles as she passed. She ignored them all, grateful that no one stopped her to ask what it was like to find Wendy's body. She'd had enough of that already.

Outside, Andrea shivered against the biting breeze. She zipped her coat practically to her chin as she started back across campus. Above her, the sky was a canopy of stars, obstructed only by a few trees and the occasional glow of a lamppost. She remembered that she needed to review her notes from her Planetary Dynamics class before turning in for the night. As an astronomy major, this was Andrea's second time around with Professor Heyer, and if experience with last semester's Theories of the Universe had taught her anything, she'd better maintain a firm grasp of the material. If you fall behind in Dr. Heyer's class, you soon find yourself adrift in the cosmos—headed straight toward a black hole.

Great. Bad puns. Like mother, like daughter. God help me.

A rustling to her right shook Andrea from her reverie. She cast a glance over her shoulder, but saw no movement on the path behind her, or in the grass and trees beyond. She couldn't help but recall her vision of Ross's murder, of the sounds in the woods. *Maybe this time, it really is an animal out there. This is God's country after all, not the city. We have skunks, possums, groundhogs, raccoons. This is a safe campus. Cameras everywhere, right? Just relax and keep moving.*

Despite her self-assurances, Andrea reached into her coat pocket and fingered the small can of pepper spray attached to her keychain. After all, how fast could she run in high-heeled boots? A faint shuffling sent her heart pounding. She whirled, ready for a confrontation.

The student center was still in sight. A group was just now filing out. Andrea breathed a sigh of relief—just before a thick arm wrapped around her mouth. With a muffled scream, she reached up with both hands and clawed at the coat sleeve as someone grabbed her legs and lifted her off her feet.

Seconds later, Andrea found herself dropped flat on her back behind a dense row of arbor vitae, pressed to the hard ground by the man kneeling over her midsection. Behind him, another held her legs together, tucked under one arm. Still a third hovered above her head, hand cupped over her mouth. All wore dark ski masks. She could feel the keychain in her coat pocket pressing against her side. If she could only reach the pepper spray—

The center man brought his hand close to Andrea's throat. Something clicked. Cold, thin metal pressed against her skin. She froze as the man spoke in a forced, raspy tone. "If you scream, it'll be the last sound you make. Now, he's going to remove his hand from your mouth and you're going to quietly answer some questions. Do you understand?"

Andrea nodded. The hand slid away.

"Good girl. Now, who did you see driving away from Wendy McConnell's house last Saturday night?"

"I just… I just saw the truck, that's it. It ran me off the road. It all happened so fast. I didn't see the driver. That's what I told the cops. Please, believe me. "

"How did you know where to find the body?"

Nearly in tears, Andrea searched for a believable reply. She couldn't think of one, so she told the truth. "Wendy led me to it. I had a… a vision."

For a moment, the man stared at her silently through the ski mask. He pressed the tip of the knife into the side of her throat. "Don't fuck with me, girl. Answer the goddamn—"

Andrea's body jolted as the man behind him dropped her legs. With a strangled grunt, he tumbled out of sight.

The ringleader twisted his upper body to peer behind him just as the third man, looming over Andrea's head, yelped and began shouting as he was dragged away by… what? Too frightened to move, Andrea gazed up at the last of her assailants. Turning his head in every direction, he held his switchblade at the ready—until it was knocked from his hand with an audible smack.

Andrea felt his weight lift from her midsection. At first, she thought he was pushing himself to his feet. It wasn't until his legs began kicking in mid-air that her mind registered it.

He was levitating.

In a panic, the man began thrashing and writhing as if struggling against an unseen grip.

"Run, Drea!"

Andrea flinched at the warning whispered in her ear—a woman's voice, familiar. "Wendy?"

"Just go!"

Andrea scrambled to her feet and stumbled toward the walkway, expecting one of the men to emerge from the shadows and tackle her to the ground. Without looking back, she ran toward the center of campus, her boots clicking and scraping against the concrete. *Don't break a heel, don't break a heel…*

A minute later, the main courtyard came into view, brightly illuminated by lampposts and garden lights. It felt safe here. She stopped to catch her breath.

The security office was only two buildings away.

And your dorm is within sight, just across the street. Take the bridge. You'll be fine.

Andrea slowed to a stop as the words entered her thoughts. She looked around, hoping to see—

"Wendy, are you here?"

"Trust me, Drea."

Reluctantly, Andrea started toward the bridge that spanned the four-lane highway and resolved to call Security from her room—after peeling off these damn boots.

***

The room was dark when she entered. Throwing the door open, Andrea slapped the light switch and made a visual sweep of the room. Satisfied that no one was lying in wait, she hastily shut the door and leaned into it as she turned the deadbolt. For several seconds, she stood with her forehead against the dull wood until she caught her breath and quelled her anxiety. Finally, she limped into the room and dropped onto her bed. Gritting her teeth, she slipped off her boots to reveal red, raw skin on the sides of her damp feet.

Andrea began sobbing. She slammed her fist into the mattress several times.

"Bastards." She stood and tore off her coat. "Fucking cock-sucking bastards!"

With a scream of rage, she kicked her desk chair aside with her heel, sending it careening into the far wall. A backhand swing scattered a short stack of used textbooks across the floor.

Andrea flinched as her phone vibrated atop her desk. In her haste to get to the memorial, she'd forgotten to bring it. Snatching up the obnoxious device, she barely resisted the urge to hurl it through the window. Instead, she looked at the screen and wondered if her night could get any worse.

"Damn it all. Not now." She swiped the screen with her thumb and pressed the phone to her ear. "Hey, Mom."

"Andrea, thank God you picked up. I had a feeling that something happened. Are you okay?"

Andrea paused. "Uh, yeah. Yeah, I'm great."

"What happened?"

"Nothing. Nothing at all. Everything's just peachy. Why do you think something happened?"

"Psychic."

Andrea sighed. With her mother well over 500 miles away, there didn't seem to be any point in worrying her. *At least not until I can sort this out. I can do this on my own. The last thing I need is my mom flying down the highway from Salem in a panic. Besides, if Wendy is protecting me…*

"Did Wendy come to you?"

"What? No, no, not at all. Uh, but I just came from her memorial and I sensed she was close by."

"Look, I know she was a wonderful person and a good friend, but she met with a violent death. Her spirit could be confused, frightened, or even angry. If she comes to you for help, please be careful. Don't let your guard down. Don't let her use you. Help her as much as you can, but not at the expense of your own well-being, okay?"

"Right." Andrea forced a perky, reassuring tone. "I get it, mom. Everything's fine. No worries."

"I'm your mother, which gives me full rights and permissions to worry. I just want you safe."

"I'm a big girl. I can handle myself."

"Not when it comes to the paranormal. I told you that before. This is new territory for you, and it couldn't have come at a worse time."

Andrea rolled her eyes. "How did your talk go?"

"It was a hoot. I had dinner with a few of the local ghost hunters, and they've invited me to join them on an investigation of some haunted locations near Salem. We're leaving in a few minutes."

"Well, have fun and stop worrying about me."

"Just call me if anything happens."

"You bet I will." After exchanging the usual "I love you's," she ended the call and tossed the phone onto the desk with a sigh. It was then that she noticed the flower lying on the windowsill—a tiger lily.

This wasn't here a second ago. Frowning, she picked it up and twirled the stem between her fingers. It brought back memories of—

"Wendy."

"Right here, Drea."

Andrea's head snapped up. She ignored her own disheveled reflection in the darkened window and stared in awe at the fiery hair and pixie face to her right. Andrea met her gaze, but found herself unable to speak. Her emotions were a tempest, scattering words and thoughts across her mind, sending a quiver through her chest.

Wendy flashed that disarming smile. "Tell me you didn't forget about me already."

Andrea burst into tears.

Wendy threw her arms around her. "I got you, babe. Those pricks didn't hurt you, did they?"

Andrea returned the embrace, resting her chin on Wendy's shoulder. She didn't know how it was possible to hold a spirit and right now, she didn't care. Wendy felt warm and alive. Finally, Andrea found her voice. "I'm sorry we were late."

Wendy pulled back and pressed her forehead against Andrea's. "What?"

Andrea trembled as she tried to catch her breath. "On Saturday night. We got lost on our way to your place. If we'd been there on time, you'd still be... still be..."

"My living, breathing, perky self?"

Andrea nodded. Wendy wiped away the tears from her face. "Hey, none of this is your fault. I know you've spent the last week beating yourself up. You can stop now." She cupped her hand under Andrea's chin, tilted her head up until their lips met, brushing softly—at first. Eventually, Wendy moved down Andrea's neck, each kiss tingling, arousing.

Andrea closed her eyes and found herself trembling again, for entirely different reasons. She drew in a sharp breath as Wendy's tongue caressed her ear.

"Does that feel alive to you?"

"God, yes," Andrea breathed. "How is this possible?"

"Don't question it, Drea. Just go with it."

"My roommate might be coming back soon."

"Nah. She's at the Dive with some of her basketball buds." Wendy reached around with both hands and squeezed Andrea's bottom.

"Wait, Wendy. Look, I don't... I can't... I'm really new at this."

"New at what, getting it on? You seemed to know exactly what you were doing on Halloween night."

Andrea flashed an embarrassed smile. "That was just... exploring."

"And when you explore, you make discoveries. I know I did. You really had me in a tizzy after that night. I couldn't get you off my mind."

"Why didn't you say something? Instead, you chased after Lance."

Wendy shrugged. "I was confused about what I wanted, or should I say who. I just wish I'd figured it out sooner."

Andrea pulled away and leaned against her desk. "What I meant was that I'm new at dealing with, you know," she gazed up at the ceiling, "God, how does my mother do this?"

"Yeah, Drea, I get it. I'm dead, an apparition. Kinda complicates things."

"I just want to know what happened and why. I already had a visit from Ross and he took me—"

"You talked to Ross? How is he?"

Andrea's shoulders tensed. "You don't know."

Wendy shook her head.

"I'm sorry. I thought since he knew about you… Ross is dead. Lance killed him on Saturday night before he got you."

Wendy's pupils dilated and continued expanding until they consumed the whites of her eyes. Andrea froze, unable to avert her terrified gaze. Instinct screamed at her to run, but she was cornered. Wendy's entire body shuddered as the color vanished from her skin, leaving it a putrid ashen.

"Wendy?"

The shriek that came next sent Andrea reeling backward. She stumbled over her office chair and crashed to the floor shoulder first. Ignoring the pain, she crawled under the desk, pulling the chair in front of her as a shield. By the time the horrific sound faded, Andrea was little more than a whimpering heap. *God help me, please. I don't want to die. Don't let her kill me, please.*

"Drea."

Holding her breath, Andrea shrank away as Wendy moved closer.

"Drea, I'm sorry I lost control. I swear it's over. Please come out."

Andrea maintained her grip on the chair—until it was yanked from her grasp. She screamed as Wendy crouched down and extended a box of tissues. Her appearance was once again normal.

"Come on, I'd die before I ever hurt you." Wendy looked away for a moment. "Shit, I guess I need to come up with a new line."

Andrea let out a laugh in spite of herself. She accepted the tissues.

Minutes later, after Wendy had finally coaxed Andrea out from beneath the desk, the pair sat facing each other in two office chairs. Wendy rolled forward and lifted Andrea's aching feet. She rested them on her lap and delicately massaged each one as they conversed.

"You never really told me much about Ross," Andrea asked. "Did you love him?"

"Like a brother. I met him when I was eleven, after my parents bought the shack. We played together every time I went there, went fishing and swimming at Stewart Lake all summer. Before his dad walked out, he built the most awesome tree house ever. We used to hang out there all the time, even into our teens. Ross and I told each other everything. I preferred being with him even more than most of my girlfriends. So naturally, I leaned on Ross after breaking off with Lance. I was distraught, but I wasn't rebounding with him."

"Everyone thought you were. By then, you weren't talking much, so I wasn't sure. When we almost collided with his truck on Saturday night, and then you said your 'ex' was at your house, I thought it was Ross. Now all of our friends think he murdered you."

"That much I heard at my memorial. Nice job standing up to Lance, by the way." Wendy ran a finger across Andrea's toes. "Better?"

"Don't stop. While you're at it, can you finally tell me what happened with him, from the top? I know you broke it off after he cheated on you over the holidays and I heard it was tense, but you shut down after that. It seemed like you were scared of something."

"Of a lot of things. The truth? Lance dumped me. It was a very civil and brief discussion. I didn't cry. I didn't even raise my voice. He wasn't worth it. I just said 'see ya later.' Part of me was relieved, because I'd started having doubts about my sexuality even before I met him."

"Because of our little tryst?"

Andrea flinched as Wendy tickled her foot. "Maybe."

"Sorry."

"Don't be, but you pulled away after that. You were still there, but distant."

Andrea paused, struggling to find the right words. "You weren't the only one with doubts. I wasn't sure if what happened that night was real or just a result of the booze. When you hooked up with Lance later, that seemed to answer the question. Afterward, I... guess I shut down a little bit, too."

"Hearts are so fragile, aren't they? Drea, you know I have an extreme personality and I'm not always rational. I wanted to prove that I liked guys so I went straight for the popular jock, the Neanderthal. In the end, I was only lying to myself. Even though we shared just one night, I thought about you a lot."

Wendy laughed softly as she continued. "I kept fantasizing that we would find ourselves alone and you would tell me how much you wanted me. Even though I felt liberated after the break up, another part of me was hurt. I suck at handling rejection. Bad enough I was confused about myself, but being cheated on and then kicked to the curb hit me hard. I was so close to calling you. So close to telling you exactly what I felt for you."

"Why didn't you?"

"I was afraid that you didn't feel the same about me and I didn't want to risk being disappointed again. So I wussed out and ended up drinking alone at the Dive that night. Worst decision I ever made… and I paid the price for it."

Classic rock music, soft at first, filled Andrea's dorm room. As she looked around for the source, painted walls darkened to wood paneling. A whirling fan grew out of the ceiling.

What the hell?

The counter that served as her dorm room's shared desk transformed into a chipped, worn bar. Andrea felt herself lifted several inches as her office chair became a barstool. The picture window stretched into a mirror covering the entire wall and reflecting everyone at the bar—except for Andrea.

The Dive.

Andrea swiveled her seat and spotted the unmistakable leonine mane of copper under the dim light of a booth near the back. She slid off the stool and started toward Wendy just as the waitress emerged from the kitchen. It was Kris, a senior chemistry major at Gustafson who worked here three nights a week. She did a double take as Wendy flagged her down.

"Can I get one more, Kris?"

"Only if you like water. I'll even throw in a lemon."

"What?"

"Sorry, honey, but you're definitely trashed."

Wendy frowned. "No, I'm not."

"Bullshit," Andrea blurted. As expected, no one heard her. With a sigh, Wendy put her hands on the edge of the table and pushed herself up until she was sitting properly. She placed her arms atop the table. "Let me prove it to ya." With that, Wendy fell sideways across her seat, knocking over her empty glass. "Or not."

Kris rolled her eyes. "Is there someone I can call to pick you up?"

"Should've been me," Andrea said.

"Perhaps I could be of assistance."

All three women looked up as Gene Brighton strolled over to the booth.

Oh, shit.

Wendy raised an eyebrow. "Professor Brighton. What're you doin' here?"

He turned to Kris. "My son's girlfriend."

Wendy snorted.

"You got this then?"

"Yes, thank you."

With a nod, Kris moved to the next occupied booth. Brighton lifted Wendy up until she sat straight. He slid into the seat across from her.

"How are you, my dear?"

She shrugged and pushed her hair away from her eyes. "Been better."

"If this is about Lance, I'm sorry."

"Lance isn't sorry about Lance."

"I'll admit he lacks maturity and discipline in some aspects of his life."

"He needs to grow the hell up. Sorry, Professor, but it's true."

Brighton smiled thinly. "No, you're right. If it's any consolation, you were my favorite. Some of these other girls he gets involved with are so utterly vapid, it's sickening."

"Vapid," Wendy repeated. "Vvvvapid. I like that word. Vapid."

"Perhaps we should get you back to your dorm."

"I live off campus." She waved languidly. "Way off campus."

"Where exactly?"

"Prahmsville. Out in the sticks about forty minutes. My parents own a little vacation home there, but I use it during the school year."

"I'll drive if you navigate."

Wendy cradled her head in her hands. "I don't know if I can do that right now."

"Well, if you give me the address, I can use my GPS."

Something about the look in his eyes triggered a creeping discomfort in the back of Andrea's mind.

"You don't have to, sir. I appreciate it, but I don't want to put you out. I can call my friend Ross or my brother, Dwight. You remember Dwight?"

Brighton nodded. "Yes, of course, he was an excellent student, but it's no problem at all. It's the least I can do." He smiled warmly and took her hand in his. "As I said, you're my favorite."

Across the table from Andrea, a pair of distant headlights shone through the window. She ignored them at first, disturbed as she was by Wendy's situation. *I wish you'd called me instead of coming here. I would've helped you forget about Lance.*

Outside, the headlights grew steadily brighter. Distracted, Andrea watched as they approached the building. *That's impossible. There's no parking in front of the Dive.* She backed away until she collided with what should have been the bar. Instead, a desk stood in its place.

The walls of the Dive dissolved into the familiar interior of "the shack."

Pushing herself off of Wendy's desk, Andrea approached the window beside the front door and peered through the open blinds as the vehicle rolled to a stop. The headlights went dark. Car doors opened and closed as silhouettes passed in front of the moonlight reflected off the windshield.

Beside Andrea, keys rattled and slid into a lock before the front door swung open.

"Now, where's the light switch?" Brighton whispered.

Wendy didn't respond. A moment later, the floor lamp revealed the reason—she was passed out in Brighton's arms. He briefly surveyed his surroundings before closing the door with his heel. Perched on the arm of the sofa, Wendy's gray tabby arched its back and stared at him.

"I suppose the bedrooms are this way."

Brighton proceeded down the hall, stopping midway. Andrea followed. Looking to the right and left, he entered Wendy's bedroom and laid her across the bed. Leaning over her, he turned her head to face him.

"Wendy?"

When she didn't stir, Brighton shook his head and pushed himself to his feet. "Just how much did you have to drink?"

Lifting her legs one at a time, he pulled off her boots and tossed them into the corner.

In the doorway, Andrea tensed. *OK, now get out.*

Instead, he leaned over Wendy and unbuttoned her jeans. Andrea drew a sharp breath and covered her gaping mouth while her girlfriend was soon stripped half-naked.

"Oh God no, you did not do this. You piece of shit!" Her ire was fruitless, of course. As it had been with Ross, she was again being forced to witness an immutable event of the past, as helpless to stop it now as Wendy had been then.

Brighton reached down and ran a finger along her thin strip of pubic hair. "Natural redhead. Definitely my favorite."

"You filthy bastard." Tears of anger and frustration clouded Andrea's eyes as she braced herself for the inevitable.

Brighton kicked off his shoes before dropping his pants. Andrea felt the heat rise in her face as he exposed his sizable erection. From his coat pocket, he produced a condom and tore open the wrapper. "Last one in the glove compartment, and fortunately for us, my dear, it's extra lubricated." He tossed the wrapper on the floor before unrolling the thin latex over his cock.

Andrea imagined herself hacking it off with an axe and shoving it down his throat. Extra-lubricated.

Climbing onto the bed, Brighton knelt between Wendy's legs and leaned over her. Andrea shifted uncomfortably, watching as he lifted her sweatshirt to her chin. "No bra… even better." He squeezed her ample breasts and massaged her nipples with his forefingers. "Lance definitely made a mistake giving you up."

Reaching around her hips, he gripped her bottom and lifted her with ease, arcing her back. Wendy groaned quietly, but did not stir even as he pushed into her.

Andrea turned toward the door to find it closed. When did that happen? She turned the knob and pulled to no avail.

"Wendy!" She slammed her fist against the door repeatedly, ignoring the throbbing in her knuckles and the cracking of hollow wood. "I don't want to see this. Please let me out!"

Finally giving up, Andrea slid to the floor. Ignoring the pain in her hand, she covered her ears against Brighton's gasps and moans and the creaking of the bed. The same bed on which Andrea and Wendy had shared that sensuous night, discovering themselves as much as one another before falling asleep wrapped in the warmth of each other's bodies.

At this angle, Brighton's overcoat blocked her view of the disgusting violation. Nevertheless, she turned her back to the scene, huddling beside the antique dresser along the wall. *God, get me out of here, please. I've seen enough. I get it now.* Her breath rasped through gritted teeth as Wendy's words came back to her. *Worst decision I ever made and I paid the price for it.*

Andrea closed her eyes. *Why didn't you come to me?* Rage, frustration, regret, guilt all consumed her until she broke down into tears. *This is what you were holding inside. This is what you couldn't tell me.*

Across the room, Brighton exhaled loudly as he finished. He pulled out and lowered Wendy. His shoulders heaved as he struggled to catch his breath. "Young lady, that was the best fuck I've had in weeks. How about you, hmmm? Oh, I see. Too stunned to reply. Well, that's quite all right."

Andrea slammed her elbow into the dresser behind her. *Son of a bitch, I'm gonna burn you.*

He slid from the bed and picked up Wendy's clothes. Clumsily, he redressed her and slipped her under the covers face down. Almost immediately, she began snoring.

The doorbell rang.

Brighton tensed. "Damn it." He gathered up his clothes and hurried into the bathroom across the hall.

Of course, now the door opens. Andrea pushed herself to her feet. She approached the bed and dropped to her knees. "I'm so sorry. I wish you came to me. I would have showed you how much I—"

The doorbell rang again, followed by the strumming of a guitar.

Andrea crept her way to the living room to find Wendy on the sofa, running her thumb over the strings.

"I didn't realize you had such a temper." She patted the cushion beside her.

Andrea clenched her jaw. A dozen sharp retorts ran through her mind, but all she could muster was, "Sorry."

"Don't be. It makes us even for my hissy fit earlier." She reached for Andrea's hand and brought it to her lips. The patchwork of bruises and broken skin across her knuckles vanished almost instantly. "Better?"

Andrea flexed her fingers. "Yeah, thanks. Who's at the door?"

As if on cue, it opened just as Brighton emerged from the hallway. "Can I help you?"

Ross stepped inside. "I came by to check on Wendy. She was expecting me around this time."

"Do you normally barge in like this?"

"I rang the doorbell twice. The door was unlocked."

"Ah, you must be Ross. Wendy mentioned you."

"And you are?"

"Gene Brighton." He extended a hand.

Ross accepted, maintaining eye contact. "You're Lance's father?"

"As much as it pains me to admit it sometimes. In fact, thanks to him, Wendy had a little too much to drink earlier. I drove her here from the Dive, but she passed out in my car. Your timing is impeccable. I just tucked her in but unfortunately, I can't stay."

"I see. Well, thank you for your help, sir."

"Of course." Brighton smiled as he stepped around Ross. He turned in the doorway. "Take care of her. She's definitely one of my favorite students."

"Douchebag," Andrea said as he closed the door behind him.

Ross hurried down the hall and into Wendy's room. He emerged a minute later, carrying her into the bathroom.

On the sofa, Wendy turned her attention to the guitar once again. "The worst is over, at least for tonight. Apparently, I started puking in bed so he took me into the bathroom and stayed with me to make sure I was okay. I was pretty wasted the next morning."

"How can you be so blithe about all of this?"

"Oh, don't think I've come to peace with what happened to me. Far from it, but I promised not to go full screaming corpse on you again."

"Much appreciated. So what happened next?"

"Ross found the condom wrapper on the floor and suspected Dr. Brighton. I had no memory of anything that happened after I left the Dive. I asked him to give me time to think, but he was always so protective of me. He actually went to Brighton's office to confront him about it."

"And?"

Wendy shrugged. "And nothing. Brighton told him he couldn't prove a damn thing and threatened a lawsuit if Ross pursued it. If Ross hadn't done that, he'd probably still be alive. He tipped his hand."

Andrea dropped onto the cushion beside Wendy. "Why would Lance agree to kill for his father?"

"Blood is thicker than water, and if other people's blood has to be shed to preserve the family honor, so be it. Big Daddy Brighton controls his boys and now, you're on their radar."

"But as far they're concerned, I didn't see anything on Saturday night. I have no proof other than visions… like this one."

"Drea, they killed Ross because he threatened one of their own. He didn't actually see me get raped, but he could put Brighton at the scene. If they even suspect you have something on them, they'll come after you again."

Andrea threw herself back and slumped her shoulders. "Ross, oh God. I still have to figure out a way to tell the cops where his body is without putting myself on the suspect list."

"I have an idea, if you're willing to help me."

"Anything you need."

"I need you."

***

As she followed Stephanie along the walking trail, Miranda wished that her own team could be here to join the investigation. The entire area was isolated from the highway by several acres of dense woods. The din of traffic had long since faded. To a city gal like Miranda, the silence was unsettling. It reminded her of the area surrounding Wendy's house, although she felt no disquieting presence here—at least, not yet. Eventually, a fork appeared in the trail.

"We're taking a right here," Stephanie said. After several steps, the paved trail ended at the edge of a wide clearing. "And we have arrived."

Standing perhaps 50 feet apart, the Abbott homes were similar in style—two-story structures with wood siding, shingled roofs, and brick chimneys. Whereas the exterior of Ruth's house had been painted a light gray, Nathaniel's was a dark burgundy. His residence was also slightly wider, a possible indication of his higher stature in the village.

"The township actually moved Nathaniel's house here because it was in the way of the new strip mall across the highway," Stephanie explained. "In its original location there's now a Pilgrim Pizza."

"Wonder if Nathaniel Abbott likes pepperoni."

Stephanie aimed her flashlight at a wooden platform almost perfectly centered between the houses. "If he's still hanging around, I'm sure he'd like to lock the developers in those and throw away the keys."

Atop the platform sat a number of pillories and stocks, all reproductions—except for one. Raising her flashlight, Miranda made her way over. The rest of Stephanie's team had arrived a few minutes earlier and were already setting up equipment inside the Abbott houses.

Miranda ran her hand along the only authentic pillory of the bunch, knowing full well that the memories of a six-year-old were unreliable at best. Could it be the same one? What are the odds? She fingered the metal lock on its right side as her thoughts turned to—

"I am so sorry, Mother."

"What?" Miranda spun to face Stephanie and squinted as night turned to day. Her friend was gone. Instead, Miranda stared at a slim teenage girl in a blue button-down blouse and long gray petticoat. The girl's high cheekbones were exactly as she remembered.

"Camille," Miranda breathed.

Her face was now clean, but the bruises were still prominent. Although free of the pillory, the girl was quivering in fear. It was then that Miranda noticed the noose lying limply around Camille's neck. Ropes secured her hands behind her back.

Miranda realized that her own wrists were similarly bound. She looked down to find herself wearing a white dress with a tan corset top. Both women stood barefoot on a gritty wooden floor littered with hay. It was high above the ground. Miranda turned to take in her surroundings. The floor was actually a horse-drawn wagon parked alongside a sturdy oak tree at the edge of a dirt road. Two ropes had been tied to a thick branch above their heads.

A crowd of onlookers surrounded them, all dressed in early colonial garb. The air was humid and redolent of body odor and manure. Miranda clenched her jaw to refrain from gagging.

"This is my fault, Mother," Camille whispered. "Please forgive me."

The floor rocked as someone climbed in behind them. It was no surprise when rough hands draped a noose over Miranda's head. She felt the knot press into the back of her neck as the rope tightened around her throat. A moment later, Camille closed her eyes as the same was done to her.

"Like me, you were given a gift from God to talk to the spirits." Miranda uttered words that were not her own. Yet somehow she knew them to be true.

"There is nothing to forgive, Camille. These people are simply too ignorant to understand."

"Blasphemy!" someone shouted.

"Cleanse us of these witches!"

"Were it not for me," Camille said. "We would not be about to die together."

"Where else would I be, but by your side? You are my daughter. I have already lost your father. What would my life be if I lose you as well? Have faith, Camille. This will be over soon, and we shall be with your father, in a place where no one can hurt us again."

The women flinched as an onlooker hurled a handful of stones at them. "Ye both shall burn in Hell, that is the only place ye'll be!"

"Silence!" A bass voice shouted from behind them. A burly man dressed completely in black stood between them. He looked at each one in turn as he spoke. "Ruth Abbott, Camille Abbott, have ye any final words?"

Camille looked at Miranda. "I love you, Mother."

The planks beneath them suddenly jerked forward. Miranda's feet dragged along the rough wood before touching thin air.

"I love you, too, Cam—"

***

Miranda gasped and reeled back from the pillory. She reached up to her throat, breathing rapaciously of the cold February air. Stephanie's hands were on her shoulders instantly, steadying her.

"Randy? You all right? What happened?"

Miranda calmed her breathing and nodded. "Let's just say I'll have a new story to tell at the conference tomorrow." She leaned against Stephanie. "I had another vision, but I didn't just see what happened. I was part of it. I was Ruth Abbott. Nothing like that's ever happened before."

"You sure you want to do this?"

Miranda choked out a short laugh. "Are you kidding? If this is the activity out here, I can't wait to get inside."

***

The first floor of Ruth Abbott's house consisted of one large room about 20 feet long by 30 feet wide. There was no power or heat, of course. Somehow, it seemed even colder in here than outside.

Beams from Miranda's flashlight revealed three rocking chairs spaced evenly around a small, crude wooden table. All were situated before a stone fireplace that consumed the middle of the rear wall. Immediately to its right, antique cookware hung from a row of pegs that ran all the way to the corner. A well-worn kitchen table and chairs, evidently handcrafted, were positioned beneath one of only three windows on the entire floor.

To Miranda's right, in the far corner, a member of Stephanie's team gripped a flashlight with his teeth while setting up a handheld infrared camera on a tripod.

"Ned, you all alone in here?" Stephanie asked.

Apparently satisfied with the angle of the camera, Ned pulled the flashlight from his mouth and readjusted his baseball cap. At fifty, he was the oldest member of Stephanie's team, and the most soft-spoken. Yet he'd managed to keep Miranda entertained at dinner with plenty of local ghost stories.

He waved toward the staircase on the left wall. "Olivia's upstairs in Ruth's bedroom with a digital voice recorder and EMF detector. Vic and Anton are opening Nathaniel's house with Pam, the curator."

After a few minutes, the trio wandered upstairs. Ruth's bedroom was the first room on the right.

Stephanie turned to Miranda and extended a hand toward the open door. "Age before beauty."

Miranda chuckled mockingly as she started toward the room. "Bitch."

"Takes one to know one."

"You're just full of clichés tonight."

"She's full of something," Ned muttered as he reached the top of the steps.

Before entering the room, something else caught Miranda's attention. Further down the hall, white sheets hung like curtains, obscuring the rest of the second floor.

"What's this?" Miranda asked.

Ned stepped up beside her. "Maintenance. Apparently, they had a leak in the roof over Camille's room. It's off limits until they fix it."

Curious nevertheless, Miranda reached out to push aside the curtain only to be confronted by a face and two hands that pressed through the sheet from the other side.

"No one here but us ghosts," the face said.

Miranda smirked. "Sorry, Olivia, but it's going to take a lot more than that to scare me. Nice try though."

Ned shook his head. "That's my granddaughter. Always sticking her nose in places she doesn't belong."

The sheets parted and the youngest member of Stephanie's team stepped out with a grin. The teenager ignored her granddad and put her arm around Miranda's shoulders. "Well, the night is still young. We'll try not to disappoint you."

"Oh, the fun already started outside."

"What do you mean?" Ned asked.

Miranda recounted her vision at the pillory. Ned and Olivia looked at each other, dumbfounded.

Olivia laughed. "Oh my God! Wherever you go, Miranda, I'm sticking with you."

"Exactly what kind of activity happens in these houses?"

"Well, see, that's the strange part," Stephanie began. "Until Nathaniel's house was moved here, neither place had any activity at all. Since then, the curator, Pam, claims that when she opens this house in the morning, the furniture in front of the fireplace is sometimes rearranged. A few times, at least one chair was knocked on its side. The door was locked and these windows don't open, so no one was in here. That's why Ned set up the camera in the corner downstairs."

"That and to see if we catch Ruth or Camille hanging around," he said.

"Or even Nathaniel," Olivia added. "He's been seen in both houses by Pam and a few tourists who thought he was an actor in costume, just staring at them in creepy silence, until he vanished into thin air."

"Voices were reported in Ruth's bedroom, too," Stephanie said. "So I have a digital voice recorder for a little Q and A session."

Miranda nodded. "So either the relocation of Nathaniel's house or its proximity to this house has stirred up activity."

"Or both," Stephanie said. "Considering old Nate sentenced Camille to hang for witchcraft before Ruth killed him."

***

It was nearly midnight by the time Nicherra returned to her dorm room. No doubt Drea was sound asleep by now. The desk lamp near the window was still on, but at its dimmest setting. Nicherra closed and locked the door as softly as possible before sliding out of her sneakers. She could see the top of Drea's head on her pillow. She was lying on her back, headphones on.

As Nicherra crept toward her bed, she risked a glance at her roommate. Her mouth dropped open. Drea's eyes were closed, phone resting on her stomach.

And she was stark naked.

"Whoa, girl." Nicherra laughed as she dropped her basketball and let it roll under the desk. "I guess you took my advice to heart, huh?"

Drea slipped off her headphones. "Hmmm?"

"About not being shy."

She shrugged. "I've always been comfortable in my own skin. How was practice?"

"Good, but exhausting." Nicherra stripped down to her underwear. "Ended up at the Dive afterwards. I should have been back an hour ago. I really need to get some sleep."

Drea nodded. "Hey, I was thinking about going streaking across campus tomorrow. Care to join me?"

Nicherra stared at her, speechless.

"That was a joke. Now who's the shy one?"

Nicherra folded her arms across her chest. "Who are you and what have you done with my roommate?"

"Oh, don't worry, she's in here somewhere…"

***

"If you're in here somewhere, can you give us a sign? Make a noise?"

Ruth Abbott's bedroom was sparsely furnished. A small bed stood in the center of the room, its headboard pressed against the wall. A battered chest of drawers stood beside a window covered with sheer curtains that were clearly new. Loose floorboards creaked as they moved about. Everyone found a secure spot and remained still.

Olivia placed her digital voice recorder near the edge of Ruth's bed. On the opposite side, the lights of the K-II meter remained dark as she spoke.

She turned to Miranda and whispered. "Maybe I should try a different approach?"

"Such as?"

Olivia raised her voice. "Wouldst thou permit us, thy humble visitors, to knoweth if thou art here?"

There was still no response from the K-II meter.

Stephanie snickered. "Seriously?"

"What? It was worth a try."

Miranda smiled, reminded of the often screwball camaraderie between her own team members. Hopefully, there would be an opportunity to join forces in the near future. She lowered herself gently onto the edge of what couldn't possibly be an original Puritan bed.

"You know that's not Ruth's original bed," Stephanie said.

"I was just thinking about that. Early colonists used straw, wool, rags or whatever they could stuff under a blanket."

"Right. That's just for display, probably a used mattress from a yard sale with an authentic fake Amish quilt over it."

As Stephanie spoke, a familiar pressure began to build behind Miranda's eyes. Something was wrong. She felt a surge of fear, but not her own. Someone else's...

Beside her, Olivia held up her K-II meter. "Are you Nathaniel Abbott? If so, can you please stand beside me?"

"You sure you want that guy next to you?" Stephanie asked.

"Are you Ruth Abbott?"

Miranda was consumed by an intense urge to call her daughter. She rose from the bed to make her way outside.

"Is Camille Abbott here?" Olivia continued. As if in response, the K-II meter erupted with activity, a frenetic flickering of multi-colored lights. "Oh my God!"

As she stared at them, a burst of pain staggered Miranda. She collapsed onto the bed as vertigo overtook her.

And the tiny lights faded away.

***

The following morning, Nicherra awoke to the sound of persistent tapping. At the desk, Drea sat naked, hunched intensely in front of her laptop. Her fingers moved lithely over the keyboard by the dim light of a floor lamp. Outside, the sun had yet to climb above the horizon. Nicherra rolled over and looked at her alarm clock. It was 5:30.

"Girl, what are you doing up at this ungodly hour?"

"Had to type something up before my day gets started." Drea stopped and peered at her screen, presumably proofreading her work. "I think I'm going to cut my last class today, I need to hit an outdoor supply store. Feel like going shopping with me?"

Nicherra flopped back down and tossed the covers over her head.

"I'll take that as a no."

***

Lance Brighton stepped out of the gym into a lashing downpour. He pulled his coat collar up over his head, lamenting the fact that his first class was at the Teeger Building on the opposite end of the campus.

"Hey, Bright Boy!"

He looked to his left just as a massive umbrella glided over his head. He clenched his jaw as Andrea Lorensen smiled up at him. Shit.

He let his coat fall back into place. "Hi."

"Hey there. You know, I wanted to catch up with you today."

His shoulders stiffened. "Oh? Why?"

"To apologize."

"For what?"

"Well, I was kinda rude at Wendy's memorial last night."

"Uh, no problem. Lot of us have been, you know, tense since Wendy died." With an exaggerated lift of his arm, Lance checked his watch. "And I hate to be rude myself, but I have a class in five over at Teeger."

"I'll walk you over."

Great. If my dad sees this... On the other hand, she clearly had no idea who attacked her last night. Lance wondered if she knew who or what had attacked them.

"I want to make it up to you."

"What?"

"For my attitude. I'm really a nice girl."

Lance chuckled. "I don't doubt it."

"Are you free for dinner tomorrow night? My treat."

"Well, I don't know. I think I have practice and then I was going to get some studying in."

"You never study on Friday night."

"How do you know?"

"I mean, no one ever studies on Friday night. Look, if you're available, they're calling for a taste of spring this weekend, over seventy degrees. Do you like stargazing? I thought maybe we could go to Stewart Lake. I have a telescope and the view is fantastic from there. No light pollution."

"Stargazing."

"That and while we're getting a taste of spring, we could… get a taste of each other."

Lance felt his face flush. He snorted an embarrassed laugh. "Wow, when you come on, you really come on."

"So come on."

Bewildered, Lance shook his head. He would never have guessed she was so aggressive or that she'd even given a damn about him. *Still, she's got a knockout smile, not to mention decent tits and a tight ass. If she's offering…* "OK, you've convinced me on the, uh, stargazing."

They reached the Teeger Building and stepped inside to exchange phone numbers.

"I'll call you tomorrow afternoon. What time does your practice end?"

"Three. Give me about an hour to clean up."

Andrea backed up toward the doors. "Sounds like a plan."

"I look forward to that taste of spring."

She flashed an impish smile as she stepped out into the rain and raised her umbrella. With a wave, she disappeared around the corner of the building.

Lance let his head roll back and exhaled loudly. He felt a pang of guilt for what he'd done to her last night. *Definitely not telling my dad about this…*

***

"Mother, wake up, please."

The pressure behind Miranda's eyes was gone. Someone spoke. *Andrea?* Miranda sat bolt upright— and immediately regretted it. *Obviously, the vertigo's still there.* She let her head drop back onto the pillow.

"Mother, are you ill?"

Miranda's eyes opened wide as panic overtook her. She faced the girl. "I have to call Andrea!"

The girl looked at her. "Who is Andrea?"

"She's my, uh…" Miranda hesitated as she studied the girl's face. Finally, she reached out and took her hand as if it were porcelain. "Camille."

"Yes?"

"My daughter."

"Of course I am."

"Of course you are." This is impossible. *My visions don't work like this.*

Camille laid her other hand across Miranda's forehead. "You do not feel feverish."

"I'm fine, sweetie." Miranda looked around the room. The lighting was dim, but not dark. It smelled of mint and burning wood. A fire was crackling nearby. *It must be morning.* She looked down at the long, pale blue nightgown that covered all but her hands and feet. *Sexy.* Camille was similarly attired. Her hair was disheveled and hung loose about her shoulders. She looked absolutely adorable.

"Sweetie? What does that mean?"

"It's… what you are—sweet. Let me look at you. After all these years…"

Camille's brow furrowed. "Years? We see each other every day."

"Right." Miranda smiled and swung her legs over the side. "Ow!" She leapt from the bed, clutching her bottom. "Something just stuck me."

Camille laughed. "It was a piece of straw, mother. They always poke through the blankets. Really, you should be used to that by now."

"I think I prefer the yard sale mattress."

"You are saying strange things this morning. I am sorry to wake you so abruptly, but…"

"What's wrong?"

Camille turned her gaze to the floor. "They are going to be hanged this morning by order of Uncle Nathaniel and the other magistrates. Sarah told me yesterday while we were out picking the mountain mint."

"Nathaniel. Your uncle. Right."

"You must be terribly tired, mother."

You ain't kiddin'. "Did you start a fire?"

"An hour ago."

"Love that smell."

Camille opened the door and led Miranda down to the main living area. The hearth was ablaze. As Camille made her way to the kitchen, Miranda stopped before the fire, taking in its warmth. On the little table before her was piled a tangle of freshly cut green plants with tiny white flowers. Mountain mint? She picked up the mortar and pestle beside them and held it to her nose. She inhaled the pungent scent and smiled. Must be.

"What time is it, Camille?"

"Nearly six of the clock."

"And who's being hanged?"

Camille sighed. "Really, mother! My friends, Betsy and Peter. Sheriff Wickett is going to hang them from the oak tree at the edge of the village, just like the others."

"I'm sorry, Camille. I'm still waking up."

"I am making tea. It should be ready soon."

Right. Coffee would still be scarce around this time. *Come on, history teacher, remember!* "They're being hanged for practicing witchcraft," Miranda guessed.

"But they did not! No one was hurt. It was merely playacting."

"And that is frowned upon."

"I know it." Rag in hand, Camille took the pot from beside the fire and brought it to the kitchen, where she poured two cups of tea. Miranda approached the kitchen table and glanced over the plates of bread, potatoes, nuts, and berries. She pointed to a pile of odd-looking nuts on a small plate.

"What are those?"

Camille looked at her with wide eyes. "They're sugar almonds. Aunt Abigail made those for us."

Miranda smiled as she popped one in her mouth. She pointed to Camille. "That's right."

Camille began breathing heavily. Her eyes glistened as she placed the teapot on the table. "I understand what you are doing, Mother; why you are acting so strangely."

Miranda paused before picking through the berries. "What am I doing?"

"You are testing me… to see if I am a witch, too!"

"What? No! No, Camille, no, no, no." Miranda rushed around the table and took the girl into her arms. "That is not what's happening at all. I promise you. I'm just not quite myself this morning. I do not suspect for an instant that you're a witch. Please forgive me."

"Thank you, Mother. I fear that this… gift we share shall someday take us to the noose as well. If anyone ever learns of it, they will surely be after us. Justice and mercy have fled as surely as the people's sanity."

Our gift? "Camille, what do you want to do this morning?"

"Peter and Betsy are still in the stocks. I promised to visit them before they are… taken away."

Miranda stepped back and shook her head. "Absolutely not. That is not a good idea."

"Mother, I promised!"

"Camille, your friendship with them could make you guilty simply by association. I believe you when you tell me they're not witches, but you know how quick people are to accuse." Miranda cupped Camille's face in her hands. "Please, stay here with me."

Camille met her gaze. Tears ran down her face as she nodded. "I shall do as you ask, Mother."

Miranda leaned forward and kissed her on the cheek. For the time being, she allowed herself to forget that she was not, in fact, Ruth Abbott—allowed herself to forget that mother and daughter were destined to die together.

***

"I can't believe how warm it is. This is just too perfect." Switching to high beams, Andrea turned onto the two-lane road leading to Stewart Lake.

"So where exactly are we doing this?" Lance asked, raising his voice over the low roar of air through half-opened windows.

"Devil's Pool."

Lance felt his stomach lurch. "Actually, I thought the lake closed at sunset."

"The state park entrances are closed, but other areas have twenty-four-hour access, Devil's Pool being one. Besides, it's the perfect spot for what we'll be doing."

Lance drummed his fingers on his knee and sighed. *Relax, she doesn't know a damn thing. If you want to get laid, just go along with it.*

Andrea looked at him. "Are you okay with this? If you're uncomfortable, we can turn back."

"What? No. I'm fine. Just… excited about stargazing."

And a taste of spring.

***

Miranda watched with feigned interest as Ruth's brother-in-law, Nathaniel, read aloud a list of names and amounts apparently owed to Ruth's late husband, Job. While researching Camille years ago, Miranda had learned that Job was a carpenter who had died of pneumonia shortly after building a number of homes in the village.

"Now we come to the larger amounts. Samuel Hawthorne, twenty-six pounds, five shillings. George Jeffrey and his brother William combined, fifty-three pounds even."

"I cannot believe you are here. I thought surely I had lost you both."

Nathaniel looked up at Miranda with a frown. "Was that Camille's voice?"

"Uh, yes. She is out gathering sticks for the fire."

"To whom was she speaking?"

Miranda shrugged. "Maybe she found someone to help her."

"Hm." Nathaniel continued reading from the ledger. "This brings the total to one-hundred and eleven pounds, three shillings—a considerable sum for you and Camille. All debts owed to Job are now paid in full."

"Thank you, Nathaniel."

"But Peter, I wanted to see you before you were taken to the oak tree, but mother would not allow it. She was afraid I might be next."

Miranda's entire body stiffened. In that moment, she realized precisely to whom Camille was speaking.

Nathaniel's brow furrowed as he rose from the kitchen table to peer through the window. For a moment, his thinning chestnut hair seemed to vanish under the harsh glare of sunlight. "I see Camille, yet no one is with her."

Miranda joined him to see two other teenagers sitting on the ground with Camille. Both had bruises on their faces—and throats. *Oh no…* As she watched, Camille reached out and tapped the girl on the arm and addressed her as Betsy.

Nathaniel whirled on Miranda, brown eyes wide with panic and fear. "She is possessed!"

"She most certainly is not."

"Then I ask again, to whom is she speaking? There is no one there."

He stormed off toward the front of the house and threw open the door. Miranda chased after him, her mind racing for a plausible excuse to appease someone from this paranoid culture.

"Nathaniel!" Miranda chose her words carefully. "Camille… is devastated over the death of her friends, so soon after losing her father. It is too much for a child to bear in so short a time. She sometimes speaks aloud as if they were still with her. Children have such imaginations. Eventually, she will outgrow it, of course."

Nathaniel glared at her. "I sympathize with her grief, but she must be stopped at once. Such conduct is idolatrous and a waste of time. Does she not have chores? One does not achieve favor with God by wasting time. Hard work is the light on the path to the Lord. I expect you to discipline her in my brother's absence, Ruth."

Miranda bowed her head. "Of course, Nathaniel. It shall not happen again." *You son of a bitch.*

"See that it does not." Nathaniel walked over to his horse and slid the documents into a pouch hanging along its side. "I must be on my way."

Miranda called to Camille and motioned for her to join them.

"I'm taking my leave of you now, Camille," Nathaniel said as Camille approached. "To whom were you speaking all this time?"

"Friends, Uncle."

"Friends?"

"As I said," Miranda chimed in. "Camille sometimes talks to—"

Nathaniel held up a hand to silence her. "My niece is old enough to answer for herself."

"I was merely playing, Uncle, to pass the time between chores. Have I done something wrong?"

"You should know better than to engage in such behavior."

Camille lowered her head. "Yes, Uncle."

Nathaniel's shoulders slumped. "I do not intend to deny you of rest between your labors. However, I advise caution in how you spend such time, Camille. Should the wrong person bear witness to your behavior, you could end up in the stocks, or worse. You know full well that Magistrate Barker has earned a reputation as a hanging judge. Even my influence may not be enough to prevent—"

Miranda stepped beside Camille and narrowed her eyes at him. "That's enough. There is no need to threaten my daughter, Nathaniel. She has done nothing to deserve such punishment."

Nathaniel nodded and mounted his horse. "If Job were here, he would put a swift end to such frivolity."

"Oh, Father doesn't mind at all."

Nathaniel regarded her with a frown. "What did you say, child?"

"I will see to the problem, Nathaniel," Miranda said sternly. "There is no need to frighten her any further."

"I am not certain she is as frightened as she should be. I shall see you both at worship." With that, Nathaniel turned his horse onto the road.

"Of course, see you at worship," Miranda called after him. *See my foot up your ass.*

"I am sorry, Mother," Camille said in a low voice. "When they approached me in the woods, I thought at first that they had been spared the noose. I did not immediately realize they were spirits."

Miranda looked away for a moment as Camille's words came back to her. *I fear that this gift we share will someday take us to the noose as well.* "So… you can talk to spirits, too."

"You told me I inherited the ability from you."

Miranda glanced at the two teenagers staring at her expectantly from beside the house. "Perhaps it would be wise if we went inside. All of us."

***

When they reached the rock outcropping that overlooked the small inlet, Andrea set aside the sleeping bag and flashlight she'd carried from her car and opened the rectangular telescope case.

"Thanks for lugging this up here for me."

"Sure." Lance set down the six-pack of beer in his other hand and retrieved her flashlight. Aiming it so she could see, he watched as she extended the legs of the tripod and steadied it on the rock. "What kind of telescope is it?"

"Expensive." Andrea lifted the instrument out of the case. "It's a reflecting telescope. This one actually has remote control guidance."

"Damn. You bought that?"

"Joint Christmas gift from my mom and dad. Even though they've been divorced for years, they both chipped in. Okay, let me set this up for you. In the meantime, can you spread out the blanket?"

"Yes, ma'am."

"Hey now, don't be a smart-ass, especially if you want—"

"A taste of spring," they said in unison and laughed.

Lance unrolled the blanket. "Now anytime someone says that I'm going to think of you."

"Is that a bad thing?"

"I hope not. Hey, this isn't a blanket, it's a sleeping bag."

Andrea glanced over her shoulder. "Right, but it unzips along the side and bottom so you can flatten it out like a blanket."

"I don't think so. It's one of those mummy style bags."

"Really? Oh, then I guess we'll just have to snuggle."

"Nice." Lance grinned as he gazed up. "Oh, wow, I haven't seen the night sky like this in a long time." He pointed up to a wispy band of stars that spanned their entire view of the sky until it vanished behind the trees. "Milky Way, right?"

"You got it, Bright Boy."

"I always used to think staring at the sky was for nerds."

Andrea motioned toward the telescope. "Well, maybe this night will change your mind."

Lance approached and peered through the eyepiece as Andrea stepped aside. After a moment, he frowned. "I don't see anything but a dark gray." He stepped back and picked up the remote control attached to the tripod. "Is there a focus button on this?" He pressed a button labeled "Align" and leaned in again for another look.

"Nope, still don't see any stars."

"Don't worry, you will."

"What?"

Lance turned just as the rock smashed into his temple. The telescope fell away as he staggered backward until his legs failed him. The back of his head cracked against the rock outcropping. High above, the Milky Way seemed to ripple and flow among the sea of stars, washing away the rest of the world with it.

***

Placing a glass of vodka on the end table beside him, Gene Brighton lifted the leg rest on his recliner and sifted through the week's mail that had accumulated in his office at Gustafson. Most of it was comprised of the usual internal memos, academic magazines, and invitations to join various professional organizations.

One item drew his attention. His name had been handwritten on the envelope. He tore open one end and slipped out the single folded paper. It was a typed letter.

Professor Brighton—

I think I may have found something that belongs to you out at Devil's Pond—a sleeping bag. It contains something that the police have been looking for, but rather than report it to them, I thought maybe you and I could come to some kind of arrangement.

I know you raped Wendy McConnell and I know Lance murdered her and Ross Benicker to save your sorry ass. The question is, have you seen Lance lately?

Devil's Pond, 9PM. This time, leave Dirk at home.

Brighton read the letter twice before he realized who had written it. The final line gave her away. He snatched his phone from the table, nearly knocking over the vodka. It was 8:15. He called Lance, but there was no answer. He didn't bother to leave a voicemail. Instead, he called his eldest son.

"Dirk, is your brother with you?"

"Nope. Haven't seen him all day. He had practice this afternoon then I think he had a date tonight."

"With whom?"

"No idea. Probably another one of his Lancettes."

"Where are you now?"

"Watching the Sixers game at Geoff's. Is everything all right?"

"Yeah, he's just not answering his phone."

"Knowing Lance, he's probably too busy playing tight-end."

"There's no need to be crude."

"Hey, if the helmet fits."

Brighton sighed. "I'll talk to you later, Dirk. Be safe."

He downed the glass of vodka and hurried to his bedroom. Opening the drawer in his bedside table, he reached for the ivory-handled switchblade. Beside it lay a .380 caliber Glock.

This time, he took both.

***

Seated before the fire, Peter and Betsy appeared no more spectral than Miranda or her daughter.

"We weren't witches," Peter contested.

Betsy reached for her brother's hand. "They lied about us."

"I know they did," Miranda said.

"How? You weren't at our trial."

"I didn't need to be there to know they lied. First of all, I doubt anyone around here is communing with the devil, and secondly, these people have no idea what a witch really is."

"You speak with such certainty," Betsy said. "You're not from this place."

"Nor from this time," Peter added.

Miranda shot a sidelong glance at Camille, anticipating her befuddled expression. Instead, the girl was staring vacantly at the fire. "Camille?"

"She can't hear us," Betsy said. "This conversation is meant only for you. You're not Camille's mother. At least, not anymore."

"How did you know?"

"We have been dead for over three hundred and twenty years. Each of us has lived three or four lifetimes since these days. Yet after each, we always regroup here."

"Why?"

Peter leaned forward in his seat. "Camille is trapped in this time, in this place. No matter how we try to convince her to move on, she can't bring herself to leave. She's been waiting all this time."

Miranda glanced at her daughter. "For what?"

"For you."

***

Hours later, Miranda sat alone in front of the hearth, twirling a stray lock of hair. Gamboling flames sent light and shadow dancing and leaping across the floor and walls. Peter and Betsy had departed to parts unknown just after dark, and Camille had cried herself into exhaustion in Miranda's arms. Eventually, she had convinced her daughter that she would feel better after a good night's sleep.

Not my daughter, Ruth's daughter. True as it was, Miranda chided herself for the thought. It had not taken long after her arrival here for her maternal instincts to kick in.   Having seen Camille's fate, Miranda wanted desperately to protect her—even though she knew her efforts would be futile.

So what the hell am I doing here? In every vision that Miranda had ever experienced, she had been nothing more than an unseen observer, a spectator to indelible events captured and preserved by time. She could no more alter their course than that of a hurricane.

Yet, this was something entirely new. For not only was Miranda interacting with the past, she was living it. That, combined with Peter's final words, raised her suspicions as to what exactly was happening to her.

Miranda leapt from her chair at a violent hammering. It took a moment for her to realize that someone was pounding on the front door.

"Ruth!"

It was Nathaniel. At this hour?

By the time he resumed his pounding, Camille appeared at the top of the stairs. "Mother, who is it?"

"I'm not sure." Miranda hurried to the door and threw it open. "What the—"

Nathaniel held up a lantern between them. It was little more than a candle inside a glass box and scarcely provided enough light to see his face.

"Ruth, I am sorry, but we are here for Camille."

"Who is 'we'?"

Another lantern moved into view from behind the corner of the house. It was carried by a burly man, taller than Nathaniel, with dark stubble. He spoke in a somber, bass voice as he held up a pair of iron wrist shackles. "Sheriff Benjamin Wickett, ma'am. I have a warr'nt for her arrest."

"On what charge?"

"Witchcraft."

"I am sorry, Ruth," Nathaniel repeated, for which he received a slap across the face. His eyes widened for a moment. "I will permit you that, but no more."

The sheriff chuckled. "A spirited woman." Just as quickly, his smile vanished. "Fetch yer daughter, please, ma'am."

Miranda stood in the doorway and crossed her arms over her chest. "No."

Wickett brushed past Nathaniel to stand within inches of Miranda. His body odor was nauseating. "If ye do not comply, I shall fetch her myself and it will not be pleasant for her."

Miranda held his gaze. "You'll need to get past me."

"Mother," Camille called. "What is the matter?"

Wickett craned his neck to look past Miranda. "Camille Abbott, yer hereby placed under arrest on the charge of witchcraft. Yer to be taken from here to be held for questioning."

"You would question her at this hour?"

"Ma'am, I will ask ye to move only once."

Miranda knew that both men could easily overpower her. Reluctantly, she stepped aside. "I will go with her."

"You shall do no such thing," Nathaniel snapped. "I would speak with you alone, Ruth. Sheriff Wickett, please be gentle. She is my niece."

Miranda moved beside Camille. "Where are you taking her?"

"To the home of Magistrate Barker. In cases such as this, it is best to have more than one judge present."

Miranda turned to her daughter. "Camille, it will be all right. Go with them. I will be along as soon as I can."

Camille shook her head. "No. I have done nothing wrong."

"That has yet to be determined." Nathaniel nodded to the sheriff who took Camille by the wrist.

"No!" Gritting her teeth, Camille drew back her other hand and punched the sheriff in the chest.

The man did not even flinch, but smiled once again. "Ye are yer mother's daughter to be sure."

Nathaniel pushed past Miranda and restrained her.

"That'll cost ye one day in the pillory," Wickett said. "Another such outburst and ye shall be whipped."

"Camille, please, don't struggle," Miranda said softly. "I will be with you soon, I promise."

Dejected, Camille said nothing more as the sheriff bound her wrists in the shackles and led her to the horse-drawn wagon outside.

"I shall be along momentarily," Nathaniel said, before closing the front door.

Miranda whirled on him. "Are the shackles really necessary?"

"Be grateful, Ruth. It was only my position as magistrate that dissuaded the sheriff from using leg irons."

"Why, Nathaniel?"

"She has admitted to speaking with the spirits of people who were hanged for witchcraft, as well as her father… my own brother. Do you realize how this could reflect upon me?"

"We discussed this! It was playacting and I have since lectured her about it. It won't happen again."

"Do not lie to me, Ruth. Camille truly thought she was speaking to ghosts. Yet we know that the souls of the dead do not remain among the living."

That's what you think, you backwards jackass.

"It is more likely that Camille has allowed herself to be tricked by Lucifer or one of his minions. It has taken the form of people she once knew and is leading her down the path to darkness."

"Bullsh—that is not true! She is merely grieving. Camille has lost many—"

"Camille has also been accused of inflicting harm through witchcraft."

"In what way?"

"Last week, while Samuel Thorpe was held in the pillory for theft, Camille went to comfort him and was struck by a stone thrown by Deliverance Bissett. It was intended for Samuel. Surely, you recall the incident? Camille and Deliverance argued over this matter and since then, Deliverance has fallen terribly ill and her condition is worsening."

Miranda shrugged. "Simple coincidence. Camille had nothing to do with that."

"No?" Nathaniel leaned forward. "That very night, Deliverance stated that Camille appeared to her in her bedroom to curse her with sickness."

"She dreamt it or her illness has made her delusional."

"We shall find out tonight. However, for striking the sheriff, Camille will be pilloried tomorrow from sunrise to sunset. There is nothing I can do to stop that. I shall see to it that she is spared a nailing, but I can only grant her so much leniency."

It took a moment for Miranda to recall that punishment in the pillory often included nailing the accused's ears to the wood.

Nathaniel stepped closer. "Know this well, Ruth. Should the court find her guilty of witchcraft, the eyes of the villagers will turn upon you. Questions will be raised as to whether you have either been ignorant or complacent."

"Camille is just a frightened girl, Nathaniel, nothing more."

"Does she have reason to be?"

***

With ten minutes to spare, Brighton turned into the parking area, headlights off. Ahead, moonlight reflected off the rear window of a silver Toyota. He parked directly beside it, facing the walking trail that led to Devil's Pool. From the driver's seat, Brighton took in his surroundings before pulling a flashlight and both weapons from the glove compartment. Separating the gun and knife, he slipped one in either pocket of his overcoat before making his way over to the Toyota.

He aimed his flashlight through the windows as he tried each door. They were locked, as was the trunk. No one was inside the vehicle. Inhaling deeply of the frigid February air, Brighton started off along the trail.

It didn't take long to realize that relying on the element of surprise would be futile, compliments of snapping twigs and crackling leaves. *She's expecting me anyway. Besides, I have no idea where she is out here.*

"Professor Brighton, nice to see you again."

He spun, panning his flashlight across the area.

"Up here."

To his left, a steep incline opened to a rock outcropping overlooking a particularly treacherous inlet of Stewart Lake. He raised his flashlight, inhaling sharply at the sight of the nude woman standing atop the hill. Matted locks of blond hair concealed her face while beads of water glistened on her fair skin.

"Andrea? Andrea Lorensen?"

Bracing herself against a tree, she placed a bare foot atop an elongated object lying on the ground before her. With a push, she sent it tumbling down the hill. Brighton darted to one side as it came to a halt at the base of a nearby tree.

"Look familiar, Professor?"

He turned his flashlight to the soiled, drenched sleeping bag. He drew back as recognition struck. It was the same bag that Dirk and Lance had used to dispose of Ross Benicker.

"Seemed like a beautiful night for a swim."

The crazy bitch actually pulled it out of the lake!

With his flashlight trained on Andrea's eyes, he slipped the switchblade from his coat pocket and started up the hill. The girl watched calmly as he approached, her expression impassive. Although the temperature had dropped considerably since sunset, she did not shiver. In fact, she appeared comfortable as she leaned back against the tree. He scanned the length of her damp body. She was definitely not concealing any weapons.

"Like what you see, Professor?"

He closed in and pressed the blade to her throat.

She did not even flinch. "Again with the knife?"

"Where is my son?"

"Nearby and safe, for now."

"Are you stoned? What could you possibly hope to accomplish? Blackmail? You have nothing on me."

She grinned. "I have nothing on at all, or didn't you notice?"

"Don't play with me, girl. I want to see my son, now."

"You will, and soon, I promise, but you need to do something for me first."

"What do you want?"

She parted her sodden hair to reveal her breasts. "I want you. Take me like you did Wendy. You know you want to."

With a coy smile, the girl snatched the flashlight from his other hand and tossed it on the ground. Clutching his wrist, she pulled his hand up and guided his fingers over her hard nipples. "It's chilly out. Warm me up."

She reached up to his knife hand and pushed his wrist down to his side. He didn't resist, but maintained his grip on the weapon nevertheless, even as she drew his head to her chest. Relenting, he pressed his lips to her damp skin.

"Just tell me one thing, Professor. Am I still your favorite?"

Favorite? It took a second for the change in her voice to register. He gazed up into her eyes—or would have, if she'd had any. Gasping, he pushed her away as all color drained from her cracked, putrid flesh. Dirty blond locks turned auburn in the stark moonlight. Blood began seeping down her forehead, dripping onto her face and breasts.

With a shriek, Brighton reeled back, left ankle twisting as the ground fell away. He tumbled down the incline before landing hard atop the sleeping bag. As he struggled to push himself up, the bag writhed and twisted beneath him. Without thinking, Brighton plunged his knife into it over and over until, finally, it lay still. He gazed up at Andrea—or was it Wendy?—but without his flashlight, it was impossible to see more than a few feet in any direction. He turned his attention back to the sleeping bag, staring at it for a moment until curiosity overtook him. He unzipped the bag.

***

Andrea found herself on her knees, leaning against a tree. She was naked and freezing. There was a phone in her hand. Someone had screamed. *Where the hell am I?*

"Drea, call the police."

"Wendy?"

She reached for the flashlight lying behind the tree.

"Wendy, what the fuck have you done to me?"

"Call them."

There was another scream. It was a man.

She aimed the flashlight down the hill. Professor Brighton was hunched over something, crying. His voice cracked as he fought to catch his breath. "You fucking bitch." He looked up at her, eyes wide with rage. He pulled something from his pocket. "He was my son! You fucking bitch!"

Andrea was shoved to the ground as the crack of gunfire erupted. She screamed as the tree splintered above her head.

"Go, Drea!"

Thorns and brittle branches scratched her bare thighs and calves as she darted into the woods. The flashlight was of little help, barely illuminating the smaller obstacles. She leapt over the thick, rotted bole of a fallen tree only to cry out as her toes cracked against a rock. Andrea fell flat on her face in a bed of pine needles. Cell phone and flashlight flew from her hands. Holding her breath to stifle any further shouts of pain, she gathered up both items and crawled toward a cluster of pine trees. Hidden by their low, sweeping branches, she turned off the flashlight and held up the phone. From the screen, the Bright Boys smiled back cheerfully. In the upper corner, there were three bars. With a mental sigh of relief, she began dialing.

"9-1-1 emergency. How can I help you?"

"I'm at Stewart Lake State Park off of Reicherstown Pike. There's a man with a gun chasing me."

"Can you speak up, ma'am?"

"No, please, I can't. Can you just send someone? He killed two others and now he's after me."

"Where in the park are you, ma'am?"

"Devil's Pool."

"I'm dispatching officers to your location."

Somewhere nearby, branches snapped. Andrea held her breath.

"Ma'am, are you still there?"

***

The morning following Camille's arrest, a cold rain fell as Miranda made her way into the center of the village. What she saw damn near brought her to tears. Camille, her head lowered in shame, stood locked in the pillory just as Miranda had seen her that first time during her childhood trip to Salem. Camille's bonnet was tilted and her drenched hair matted against the wood. A group of five gawkers had already gathered several feet from the pillory.

"Camille Abbott!" a woman called. "Who would have thought ye to be a witch, coming from such a God-fearing family?"

"Did you curse Deliverance with sickness?" a young man taunted. As Camille looked up, he hurled a stone. She cried out as it struck her just below her right eye.

"Stop it!" Miranda charged toward the group, sending most of them scattering. There were gasps and a scream as she tackled the man to the mud. He looked up at her with wide eyes as Miranda pummeled him repeatedly in the face, each strike accenting her words.

"She is not a witch, you punk!"

Hands grabbed her arms and hair and dragged her away from the man. He rolled over onto his side and wiped the blood from his lip.

"What has occurred here?"

Miranda looked up as a familiar figure stomped through the rain towards her.

"She attacked this man, Sheriff," an older woman said, "for calling her daughter a witch."

"She insulted him using a strange word," another added. "Perhaps a word witches use."

Wickett hauled Miranda to her feet with one arm and sneered. "There is one certain cure for a willful woman." He nodded at two men, including the young one she had attacked. "Help me get her to the post."

He smiled. "With pleasure."

"Mother!" Camille called.

"Don't worry about me, Camille." *It will all be over soon anyway.*

The sound of her daughter's sobs carried all the way to the whipping post. The two men pinned her arms to either side while the sheriff clamped her wrists.

"Strip her to the waist while I fetch the whip."

Miranda gritted her teeth as the men grabbed and tore at her blouse and waistcoat until all that remained were the sleeves. Several onlookers laughed. Both men smirked and lowered their lascivious gazes to her bare breasts. Fearing the pain to come, Miranda closed her eyes and leaned her forehead against the damp, weathered wood. She shivered as frigid rain like ice crystals pelted her exposed flesh.

The sheriff returned and moved beside her. He brushed the whip against her back. "As yer of Nathaniel's family, I will give ye only ten lashes for yer outburst... and two more for making me stand out here on this wretched day."

***

Brighton fell against a tree, taking weight off his injured ankle. With his coat sleeve, he wiped sweat from his nose and chin. *I heard her cry out in pain. She couldn't have made it far if she's hurt.*

His chest quivered as he thought of Lance bleeding out in the dirt. He leaned forward, burying his face in his hands.

"Am I still your favorite?" It was a whisper on the breeze. Brighton drew himself up, fearing the sight of Wendy's cadaverous face hovering over him, but there was only darkness.

No, that was an optical illusion, a trick of the moonlight. *There are no ghosts here, only a demented girl. Focus!*

He glanced around in every direction, looking for even the slightest hint of light or movement.

Finally, he saw it. A small point of white light appeared in his peripheral vision. He hunched low and watched it move from side to side, disappearing and reappearing behind tree branches. She was close. With a grunt, he staggered toward her. The light fell out of view. No matter—he'd marked her. Creeping within reach of the tree, he could see the light on the ground. In one swift motion, he bent back the branches and leveled the Glock.

Andrea was gone.

"Ma'am, are you still on the line?"

Dropping to one knee, he picked up his phone and ended the call. *Very clever, lifting my phone.* He estimated 15 to 20 minutes before the police arrived. *I was forced to chase her. She seduced my son and brought him here to murder him. By the time I showed up, she had already stabbed him to death. You must understand. I had no choice.*

No choice but to kill her.

Swiping the screen with his finger, he located the flashlight app and turned it on. Something shuffled between the trees nearby. Brighton flexed his fingers around the grip of his gun and slowly circled the cluster of evergreens. He brought the light to bear on a raccoon scaling a nearby tree. The animal narrowed its beady eyes.

With a sigh, Brighton lowered his phone and backed away—just as a handful of pine needles were thrust into his eyes.

***

By the time Brighton fired two wild shots into the woods, Andrea was doubling back toward the parking area, guided by Wendy's disembodied voice.

"Stop."

Andrea halted, nearly tripping over her own bloody feet.

"Shine your flashlight ahead."

It was the hill that she'd stood atop earlier, when Brighton had arrived.

"Damn it, Wendy, what the hell have you done to me? Where are my clothes?"

"On the rocks overlooking the water, near your telescope."

Andrea started toward the lake.

"No, Drea, there's no time. You need to get out of here."

"You say that now after almost getting me killed."

"You know I'd never let that happen."

Ignoring her, Andrea limped her way along the top of the incline and back to the spot where she had set up her telescope. Her clothes were piled on the ground beside it. After clumsily dressing herself, Andrea reached into the pocket of her jeans and retrieved her keys.

She turned toward the trail leading to the parking area. After three steps, she turned back and stared at her telescope. "I can't leave it behind."

"Drea, please just go."

"I can't leave it, Wendy."

Switching off the flashlight, Andrea began breaking down the telescope. She was more than able to do so even in complete darkness. "I agreed to help you and you took advantage of me. You want to do something for me? Go distract Brighton. Keep him off of me until I get my shit together and get to my car."

"I'll do what I can, but I can feel myself fading. This has taken a lot out of me."

"You weren't the one running around naked in the woods with some psychopath trying to kill you. I'm filthy. My feet have gone numb and I've got cuts and scratches in places where they have no business being. So what are you saying, you're just going to leave me like this?"

There was no response.

"Wendy?"

***

By the time Miranda was released from the whipping post, she could barely stand. The onlookers had gone, either because their day's drama had ended or the weather had chased them away.

The freezing rain had all but numbed her entire upper body. Miranda could no longer feel what had been the unbearable sting of a dozen lacerations across her back.

Someone moved beside her. She looked up to see Nathaniel unlocking the shackles. Her lifeless arms flopped to her side and she fell to her knees. Gingerly, he placed his arms under hers and lifted her to her feet. She leaned into him and he was careful not to touch her back.

"Come, Ruth. My carriage is just a few steps away," Nathaniel said. He placed his hands on her upper arms and guided her away from the post.

"I want to see my daughter."

"Ruth, I must tend to your wounds."

"Take me to her, damn it."

"You are a strong woman, Ruth, but curb your tongue, please. Else they will clap your head in a brank."

In front of the pillory a moment later, Miranda shrugged off Nathaniel and went to Camille. The girl's head was lowered once again, chin pressing against the wood. Her bonnet had slipped off and lay in a puddle. Miranda put her hands on both sides of Camille's shivering face and lifted her head. She parted drenched hair to reveal an expression of hopelessness.

"Mother," she whispered.

Miranda pressed her forehead against Camille's. "I'm here."

"I can no longer feel my legs. I fear I will not be able to stand the full day."

"Nathaniel, can you not release her?"

He shook his head. "She must serve her sentence until sunset."

"Exposure to the cold for this long could cause hypo—could make her extremely ill."

"The sky is beginning to clear and the afternoon sun will warm her."

Camille let out a low moan as she shifted her weight. "I am sorry for your whipping, Mother. Perhaps it would have been best if you had stayed home."

"You are my daughter. I will not leave you to these animals. It is not you who need apologize."

"The magistrates have decided to put me on trial tomorrow morning."

"There was no time to tell you, Ruth," Nathaniel interjected.

"You will not face them alone. I will be there, Camille. Be strong today, for tonight, you will be with me in front of a warm fire."

"And tomorrow I will be hanged."

Miranda stared into her daughter's eyes, her mind racing for words of comfort. She was painfully aware that any assurances she offered would be lies, yet one thing remained true.

"You are not a witch."

***

Facing the blazing hearth, Miranda sat atop the small table in her damp petticoat. Leaving her back exposed, she had tied an apron around her neck to cover her chest. Miranda inhaled through gritted teeth as Nathaniel began treating her wounds with an odorous ointment. Apparently, in addition to serving as a magistrate, Ruth's brother-in-law had been trained as a physician.

"Pity." He stepped around her and retrieved a long, damp cloth that he had hung by the fire. "For such a lovely back to be permanently scarred so."

Miranda merely stared at the crackling flames. Though sufficiently warmed, she was drained physically and emotionally. She had no idea why she was still here. She wanted nothing more than to end this vision and return to her own time, her own life… to Andrea. *What's left for me to learn here? I know how this ends…*

"I must wrap this cloth around you."

Miranda didn't move, nor did she resist as Nathaniel untied the apron and let it fall to her lap. He moved behind her and pressed the warm, moist fabric to her back. Reaching under her arms, he slid his hands across her breasts. He squeezed them gently as his lips caressed her neck.

Miranda leapt to her feet. "What are you doing?"

"Ruth, you have been alone, without husband, for many months. Since Job's death, you and I have become closer, and… I have become rather enamored with you. It was unexpected. One day, I cannot recall exactly when, I saw you in a different way, felt for you in a different way."

"Well, that's flattering, but you're a married man."

"To a woman who is colder than freezing rain. Abigail and I have scarcely shared intimacy in years."

"I'm sorry, Nathaniel, but this is hardly the time or place. My daughter stands humiliated and afraid for her life, accused of a ridiculous crime she didn't commit."

Nathaniel moved closer, forcing Miranda into the corner of the room. She placed her hands against the walls behind her to prevent her throbbing back from pressing against the rough plaster. He still held the cloth in his hand, mottled with thin, bloody lines from her wounds.

"I can help her," he said. "If you relent to me just this once, I can wield some influence with Magistrate Barker, perhaps even ensure the witchcraft charges are dismissed."

"You are the one who betrayed her in the first place. Why should I trust you?"

"Because I am the only hope you have."

"Your carriage driver is waiting."

"He does not care how long I am here. He is paid to wait."

Nathaniel tossed the cloth onto the nearest chair and moved closer. Miranda sidestepped, crossing in front of the fire. She snatched up the apron from the table and held it to her chest.

"You accuse my daughter of witchcraft while you entertain thoughts of adultery. As you try to take advantage of a distraught and injured woman, Nathaniel, ask yourself who is more the sinner. Perhaps you're not above a day in the pillory."

Nathaniel charged after her. Miranda backed away until she collided with the kitchen table. Pots and plates rattled. *If I wasn't wearing this damn petticoat dress, I'd kick him in the gonads.*

"You feign weakness when convenient, Ruth," he seized her by the shoulders and pulled her close. She recoiled at the stench of his breath. "But I know better. You would do well not to refuse me."

"Let go of me!" Miranda tried to push him away. Instead, he shoved her until she landed on her back atop the kitchen table. Miranda screamed and winced as the pain seared through her. She arched her back and tried to turn her body as Nathaniel reached behind her to untie the waistline of her petticoat.

Without thinking, she reached across the table and grabbed an iron skillet. With a roar, she swung and backhanded Nathaniel across the temple. He staggered to one side long enough for Miranda to push herself off the table.

"Filthy witch!" He advanced on her, fists balled.

Miranda ran toward the door, but Nathaniel was faster. Halfway across the room, he grabbed her around the waist and yanked her backward. Miranda twisted, slamming an elbow into his stomach. With a grunt, Nathaniel doubled over. She wrenched herself free of his grasp and spun, bashing his head repeatedly with the skillet until the bottom of it was stained with blood. Nathaniel crumpled to the floor, unmoving.

Miranda fell to her knees. "Nathaniel?" She turned him over and peered into his open, lifeless eyes. *Oh, shit...*

The front door burst open. The carriage driver, a husky man with several teeth missing, dashed into the house and stopped. After a moment, his eyes went wide at the sight of blood pooling around Nathaniel's head and the half-naked woman looming over him with a skillet.

At that moment, Miranda realized that on October 13, 1692, Ruth Abbott had sentenced her daughter—and herself—to death.

*****

Andrea ducked behind one of the picnic tables along the edge of the parking area and turned off her flashlight. Sirens in the distance grew steadily louder. No doubt Brighton heard them, too—wherever he was. Her car was maybe fifty feet away. His was parked beside it.

I should just wait here until the cops show up. Andrea tapped her fingers lightly on the metal telescope case. *Maybe I should get this into the trunk. Mom and dad will kill me if anything happens to it.*

Staying low, Andrea hugged the case to her chest and crept toward her car. Although flip-flops were not exactly stealthy, she was grateful for the thin layer of plastic between her soles and the sharp gravel. *Couldn't have dressed me in sneakers, Wendy?*

She was halfway to her car when the crack of gunfire sent a jolt through her. Andrea froze, scanning the area until she spotted Brighton limping out of the woods from the opposite side of the dark parking area.

Without a word, he continued firing wildly. Screaming, Andrea dropped to her knees and raised the metal telescope case as a shield. "Wendy! Help me, please!"

Nearby, a car engine roared. Wheels spun in the gravel. Brighton grunted as if the wind had been knocked out of him. A moment later, Andrea cringed as wood and bone cracked. Glass shattered. Screeching sirens closed in. Red and blue lights flashed through her clenched eyelids.

By the time Andrea peeked around the telescope case, three patrol cars had pulled into the lot. Their headlights revealed the slumped body of Gene Brighton, crushed between the rear bumper of his own car and the thick bole of a nearby oak. There was no one behind the wheel.

A pair of officers ran toward her, the beams of their flashlights bobbing in her vision. She rested her head against the case, cradling it in her arms. Her fingers slid across its rugged shell until they found the bullet hole.

I should've listened to you, Mom.

***

Miranda blinked as her eyes adjusted to the darkness. Flashlights illuminated the floor around her. She was kneeling in the same exact place, yet Nathaniel's body was gone. There was no blood, no blazing hearth, no tapping of light rain against the windows. Her hands were empty. She was fully clothed—jeans, boots, winter coat. The room was cold.

"Randy?"

Miranda raised her head as Stephanie lowered herself to one knee. Ned and Olivia stood behind her.

"Randy, are you back with us?"

Miranda nodded, too enervated to speak right away. Stephanie put her arms around her and helped her to her feet.

Miranda gasped and arched her back.

"What's wrong?"

"Feels like my back is on fire."

Olivia stepped around behind her. "Let's have a look."

With some assistance, Miranda slipped off her coat.

"Oh my God, there's blood coming through your shirt."

Stephanie and Ned joined Olivia, all aiming their flashlights at Miranda's back.

"Randy, can we lift up your shirt?"

Miranda bowed her head. "Yeah."

She felt the material pull away. Cold air swept across her back. Both women gasped.

"Are those scratches?" Olivia asked.

"More like lashes from a whip," Ned replied.

"Randy, we need to get you to the hospital."

Miranda shook her head. "I'll be fine, Steph. If we do that, there'll be too many questions. I'd rather just go back to the hotel and take care of it."

"You're not fine judging by what we're seeing," Olivia said. "There are at least ten lacerations across your back."

"Twelve, actually," Miranda said.

"Would you mind if I took a picture?"

"Sure, why not? It's evidence."

Stephanie moved beside Miranda. "Wait. You know how this happened don't you?"

"How long was I out of it?"

"About twenty minutes. We caught some of it on the IR camera. You collapsed on the bed for a few seconds then you got up and walked down the steps. I realized you were having a vision when you didn't respond to us.

"You wandered around down here for a little while, sat at the kitchen table, sat in front of the fireplace and even went back outside to stare at the pillory for a while. Then you knelt down here and snapped out of it. Freaked us out."

"Mostly because you didn't utter one word the entire time," Ned added. "Been ghost hunting for over fifteen years and I've never seen anyone in a God's honest trance before."

"Happens to me all the time." Miranda pointed a thumb over her shoulder. "Hey, I'm starting to freeze back there."

"Oh, God, I'm sorry." Olivia lowered Miranda's shirt. "At the very least, you should get some antibiotic ointment and dress those wounds."

Miranda nodded as she put her coat back on. "Steph, would you do the honors?"

"I'll do my best. Ned, you and Olivia can continue investigating if you want. Can you let the rest of the team know that Randy and I had to leave? We'll catch up at the conference tomorrow."

Trudging back toward her car a few minutes later, Stephanie gave up trying to persuade Miranda to go to the Emergency Room. "Well, can you at least tell me what happened back there? What did you see in your vision?"

"The answer to a thirty-six-year-old mystery. I'll explain on the way."

***

With her shirt in her lap, Miranda sat in a lotus position near the edge of the bed as Stephanie emerged from the bathroom with bandages and a warm, soapy cloth. Miranda peeked over her shoulder just as Stephanie stopped a few feet away, mouth agape.

"What's wrong?"

"Oh, wow. That is just crazy."

"What?"

"The marks on your back are healing right before my eyes."

"Seriously?"

"I shit you not."

"Let me see." Miranda unfolded her legs and slid from the bed to stand before the mirror above the desk. She turned and stared at her reflection, watching the lacerations shrink to thin red lines before completely vanishing.

"Good thing we took a picture," Stephanie said. "Although I am disappointed. I was really hoping to get your bra off."

Miranda chuckled and shook her head. She dropped into the office chair and sat back. There was no pain—at least, not physically. As she thought of Camille, Miranda began twirling a lock of her hair. Her vision blurred as tears welled up.

Stephanie dropped the bandages on the bed and sat down. "You all right? I mean, from what you told me in the car, I know you went through hell tonight."

Miranda leaned forward, elbows on her knees. Her voice quivered. "What was twenty minutes to you was days to me. I lived Ruth's life. Three hundred years ago, I had a daughter, Steph. A sweet, wonderful, innocent girl."

Tears ran down Miranda's face. "And they hanged her. Those bastards brutalized her and hanged her because she had my ability."

"That wasn't your fault, or Ruth's. It was Puritan society. You know that. You teach it every year."

"It's one thing to discuss it in class. It's something else entirely to live it, to know that you were there with a different name, a different face. I can't help but wonder if Camille's soul moved on to someone in my life today. Is she my daughter again now?"

"Well, you did say at dinner that Andrea's just beginning to exhibit your abilities."

Miranda stood and yanked open the top dresser drawer. She pulled out another shirt and slipped it on. "I need to go back there."

"Where, Ruth's house?"

"And maybe Nathaniel's."

Stephanie shot to her feet and stood between the bed and the dresser, blocking Miranda's exit. "No."

"I want to know more."

Stephanie crossed her arms over her chest.

"I need to see Camille again."

"I don't care."

"She's my daughter, damn it!"

"And there it is. That obsessive streak. You haven't changed in all these years. Once a vision becomes personal, you can't let it go. You came away from that place with wounds like I've never seen in any haunting. Do you really think I'm going to take you back there?"

"I'll find it myself. My car has a GPS."

"I'll call Pam, the curator, and tell her to close up, lock the doors. You won't get in."

"I don't need to get in the houses. I can just go to the pillory again."

Stephanie took a step forward until she was practically nose-to-nose with Miranda. "You stubborn blonde bitch, I will use both of our bras to tie you to that office chair if you don't sit down."

For several moments, the women merely glared at each other in tense silence before Miranda's mouth twisted into a wry grin. "You would do that."

"You know I will. You may be quicker, but I guarantee you I'm stronger."

"You're threatening when you're beautiful."

"Are you going to behave?"

"Bully."

"It's for your own good."

Miranda's shoulders slumped and she leaned against the dresser, finally relenting to the fatigue that had settled over her soon after her visions had ended. "You're right, I know."

Stephanie put her arms around her and gently pulled her close. "We were like sisters once."

"We still are, Steph. If I learned anything tonight, it's that time and distance do not matter when you love someone."

"Will you be okay to stick around the conference tomorrow?"

Miranda nodded. "I have two discussion panels in the morning. I'll probably grab lunch before hitting the road. I'd like to stay until Sunday, but I want to get home in case Andrea needs help. Although, she hasn't called or texted me yet."

"Give her a shout before it gets too late."

"I talked to her before we went to dinner, I don't want to suddenly become that mom when she's twenty. I'll call her tomorrow before I hit the road."

***

Seated in the ambulance, blanket draped across her shoulders, Andrea flinched as the EMT gently swabbed and bandaged several cuts on her legs and feet.

"Sorry," he said. "I know some of these sting like hell."

"No worries. This is the best part of my night."

"In that case, I really am sorry."

Andrea gave him a slight smile before leaning her head back. "Thanks for your help."

She stared at the ceiling, unsure what was worse—conjuring up a story for her mom or the sheriff. Better think fast, he's coming back!

"Hot chocolate?"

The ambulance driver appeared in the doorway. She held out a Styrofoam cup. "I usually carry a thermos on board in the winter."

Andrea thanked her and accepted the cup just as the sheriff stepped up beside the driver.

"Well, Ms. Lorensen, we meet again. How ya holdin' up?"

"Just peachy."

"You always seem to be where the action is, so can you tell me what happened out here?"

"I came here to stargaze off the rock ledge overlooking Devil's Pool."

"Stargaze." The sheriff nodded. Andrea knew this was going to be a hard sell. "Alone?"

"Yep."

"That's pretty brave for someone who doesn't know the area."

"You mean brave for a woman?"

"Wasn't implying that. We have bears in these woods and they don't all hibernate in the winter. We get a warm spell like this, they tend to roam."

"Huh. Didn't think about that."

"Anyway, you came out here to stargaze."

"Am I getting my telescope back?"

"Once we pull the bullet from the case and match it to the weapon found near the man who was run over, yes. For now, I can tell you that it looks like the telescope itself was unharmed. Good thing you have a metal case."

Andrea's shoulder slumped in relief.

"Now, as to what happened…"

"Uh, yeah, about that." She rubbed her hands together nervously. "Well, it's all a bit of a blur now. So, a few minutes after I set up my telescope on the rock ledge, I heard another car pull up. That's when I started thinking that coming out here alone was a bad idea, you know? I could hear footsteps approaching so I turned off my flashlight and kept quiet.

"Then, uh, someone came out of the trees at the other side of the ledge. He had a flashlight, which was how I knew it was a guy, and he had some kind of sack over his shoulder. He lowered it to the ground then kicked it off the ledge. I heard it hit the water. Then he just turned and walked off."

"Was it the man who shot at you?"

Andrea nodded and took a sip of the hot chocolate before continuing. The words tumbled out of her mouth. "I thought he was gone so I snuck over and shined my flashlight into the water, but I couldn't see what he dumped in there. But I can tell you that wasn't the only thing he kicked into the lake."

"What else?"

Andrea reached up and lifted several locks of her damp hair. "Me. While I was leaning over the ledge, I got kicked in the ass and dropped right in. I saw it then. It was a sleeping bag—and it wasn't empty."

"We found a sleeping bag in the woods not far from Devil's Pool. Same one?"

"I don't think so."

At that, the sheriff turned and called out to the other two cops. "Guys, we might have another body bag in the drink. Call Drayton. Tell him to get in his wet suit and get over here."

By now, Andrea's hot chocolate was cold. The ambulance driver held out a hand for the cup. "Sheriff, I think it's time we get her to the hospital."

"I want to hear how this ends, don't you?" He looked at Andrea.

"Well, uh, I swam about twenty feet over to the shore line, you know, hoping to get away from the guy, but he was right there as soon as I ran out of the water. I recognized him immediately. Professor Gene Brighton. He's a dean at Gustafson."

"Was he with anyone else?"

Andrea shrugged. "Not that I saw. Anyway, he, uh, grabbed me by the hair and we fought. His phone fell out of his pocket. I kicked him in the ankle and he let me go. Then I grabbed the phone and ran away. I couldn't see where I was going." Andrea waved a hand over her legs. "Hence these lovely marks. He took a few shots at me, but I managed to hide long enough to call you guys. He had me cornered at one point, but I threw pine needles in his eyes, which gave me enough time to double back, grab my telescope and try to sneak back to my car. That's when he caught up with me and started shooting again. I hit the ground and ducked behind my telescope case. Didn't open my eyes again until you showed up. I thought he was going to kill me."

The sheriff raised an eyebrow. "So, a man just dumps a dead body in the lake, pushes you into the water, chases you through the woods with a gun, and you decide to go back for your telescope?"

"I'm an astronomy student, Sheriff, I have my priorities. Besides, it did save my life."

***

It had been nearly midnight by the time Andrea was discharged from the emergency room. The sheriff had shown up to tell her that her car had been impounded and searched. As nothing suspicious had been found, he'd kindly driven her to the station to claim both car and telescope. The telescope's case, however, had been locked in the evidence room.

Before she departed, the sheriff took her into his office and closed the door. He motioned for her to sit as he rounded his desk and dropped into his chair. "You're going to see all this in the press soon enough. The body in the water was Ross Benicker. The other one was Lance Brighton. Right now, it looks like both were stabbed with the same knife. We found a switchblade in Professor Brighton's coat pocket. It had blood on it. My finely honed police instincts tell me there's a connection to Wendy McConnell's murder. I'm investigating that."

Andrea clenched her jaw and said nothing further, for the sheriff's words had brought all the closure she needed.

"Down the line, I might have more questions for you, and possibly your mother. I just wanted you to be aware."

"Are we suspects?"

The sheriff shook his head. "Not at all, but at the same time, I don't believe in coincidences. You're the only connection in both cases. I wonder why that is."

Andrea shrugged. "Apparently, I've become popular with dead people."

***

The following afternoon, while Nicherra was at basketball practice, Andrea sat at her desk staring at images of nebulae on an astronomy website. For nearly twenty minutes, the cosmic panoply of colors and shapes went unseen. Her mind may as well have been in another galaxy as she struggled to come to terms with the surreal events of Friday night. *How the hell can I focus on homework after all this shit? For that matter, how can I return to a normal life at all?*

Her screen went dark, disrupting her fretful reverie—and reflecting a familiar face just over her shoulder. This time, Andrea felt no emotion, only apathy. She didn't even bother to turn around. "You said you cared about me."

"I do, Drea."

"You damn near got me killed."

Wendy moved beside her. "I told you, I would never let that happen."

"No, you just used me and when you got what you wanted, you left me there, naked and vulnerable."

"I saved your life. Brighton would have killed you."

"You're the one who put me in harm's way to begin with!" Andrea slammed the lid on her laptop. "Actually, to be honest, I let you do it. I invited you to risk my life, and now more people are dead and once again, the sheriff finds me at the scene. I had to bullshit my way through most of my story."

"Drea, he's not going to charge you with anything."

"What about that threatening note you made me type up to Professor Brighton?"

"Gone. No one will ever find it."

"Just like that. It's so easy for you. I have to live with what happened last night. You don't."

Wendy dropped to her knees in front of her. "Drea, before all this happened, before Lance, you and I started something beautiful. Even though it was only one night, I never stopped thinking about you and my instincts told me that you felt something, too. I regret that we never had the chance to explore that, but please… don't let it end this way."

"I don't know what to say to you, Wendy. I need time to sort this out."

Wendy nodded and lowered her gaze. "If you decide you don't want to see me again, I'll understand, but I hope you can eventually forgive me."

Andrea remained silent for a moment, using every ounce of willpower to hold back her tears. "And if I do, how would I find you?"

Wendy stood and held out a single tiger lily.

"Leave one of these nearby and I'll find you."

The flower dropped onto Andrea's lap. She picked it up and twirled it between her fingers.

For nearly an hour, she cried alone.

***

Saturday morning's discussion panels provided a pleasant contrast to the previous night's ordeal. After a final meal with Stephanie and her team, Miranda stopped in the hotel lobby and called Andrea. She stifled a surge of panic when there was no answer.

"Hey, it's Mom. I'm leaving Salem now. It's about one-thirty. Just checking in to make sure you're OK. If you call me and I don't pick up, leave a message. I'll pull off at a rest stop and call you back. Otherwise, I should be home around ten, barring any problems. OK. Love you. Bye."

Of course, there were problems, and 10PM turned into 1AM, compliments of southbound road construction, a car fire, and two accidents, one of which involved an overturned tractor-trailer.

By the time Miranda reached the outskirts of Baltimore, her head was threatening to explode. She parked across the street from her row home, the only vacant spot available. Before stepping out of the car, she checked her phone. No new calls or text messages. With a sigh, Miranda unloaded her luggage and wheeled it across the street to her house.

Once inside, she turned on the lights, slipped off her boots, abandoned her luggage by the door and went straight for the bathroom. After a hot shower, she collapsed face first onto her bed.

***

Awareness slowly intruded into her consciousness as her bare arms and legs tingled against the chill. She curled into a ball, shivering. No, shaking. Someone was shaking her, yet she lacked the energy to even open her eyes—until an obnoxious buzzing erupted beside her head.

With a gasp, Miranda pushed herself up and turned onto her back. The blanket and comforter were gone. The bed rocked from side to side. Miranda leapt to her feet and switched on the lamp atop her bedside table.

All movement ceased. The covers were piled on the floor at the foot of the bed. Miranda slapped the button to silence the alarm clock, noticing that it was just after 3AM. Her bedroom was freezing, each breath a puff of white steam. The familiar pressure behind her eyes, mild when she had first woken, was intensifying.

She had a visitor from the other side. But who and where?

Ignoring that for the moment, Miranda scooped up the tangled covers and tossed them onto the bed on her way to her dresser. She slipped into jeans and a sweater before reaching for the closest pair of shoes.

"Ruth."

Miranda paused. The voice had been close by, somewhere in the room. She waited, but heard only the popping and creaking of the walls and floor. Then came the heavy breathing and a woman's soft sobbing.

The alarm clock!

Miranda stood by the bedside table and crouched down. She leaned close to the speakers. A man's voice, low and threatening. His words were barely discernible, but a few were clear.

"Waiting... move on... soul... return... mother... Camille."

It was Nathaniel. Shit.

"Mother?"

Miranda shot to her feet and nearly stumbled into the table. Across the room, Camille stood by the window. Her appearance was the same as when Miranda had met her for the very first time—locked in a pillory.

"He is here, Mother," she whispered, shivering. "I could not stop him."

Before Miranda could utter a word, the bedroom door flew open. Something gripped her ankles and pulled. She fell forward, her face bouncing off the edge of the bed before hitting the floor. She yelped as unseen hands dragged her from the room.

Miranda clawed in vain at the hallway carpet before grabbing the spindles of the railing. Her limbs and torso stretched until the pain was unbearable. With a roar of agony, she relinquished her grip. Her body was violently turned and yanked down the stairs, head and chest bouncing off each step until the wind was knocked out of her. Finally, Miranda slid to a halt in the center of her living room. Her entire body ached as she rolled over onto her back and stared up at the ceiling. Dark lines began to appear as if burning themselves into the paint. As she watched, the lines coalesced into letters and those letters formed one word.

WITCH.

***

She trudged through the barren field, her shoes waterlogged from the recent storm. Andrea pulled her raincoat tighter around her shoulders and chest. She stopped and took in her surroundings.

What is this place? How the hell did I get here?

Bare trees and evergreens bordered the edge of the field behind her. There were no structures in sight to offer her shelter from this cold, damp morning. Overhead, threatening clouds drifted past, tearing apart and merging again, casting a gray pallor over the landscape.

Ahead of her, the field ended at what appeared to be a dirt road. A single oak, ancient and sturdy, stood apart from the other trees. Its branches were raised toward the heavens as if to welcome whatever onslaught nature was about to unleash.

All, but one. The lowest branch arched up from the center of the bole and jutted straight out over the road.

Something hung from that branch. As Andrea drew closer, she realized it was someone. Suppressing a shiver, she rounded the oak and stood in the road. It was a woman, topless. Her back was bloody from a recent whipping, the waistline of her long dress stained red. The woman's blonde hair, darkened either from sweat or rain, was strewn about her shoulders and back. Slowly, Andrea stepped around the woman's bare feet and peered up at her face.

She drew in a sharp breath. Then, from behind her, "Mother?"

Andrea spun to face a young girl in Puritan attire. She appeared to be in her late teens. Her dirty blonde hair was pinned up and tucked under a bonnet.

"What did you say?"

"She is my mother."

"Like hell she is! Who are you?"

"My daughter."

Andrea looked back at her mom. Her eyes were open and her hand outstretched, reaching for—whom?

The Puritan girl brushed past Andrea and clutched her mother's hand.

Andrea shook her head. "No. Mom, it's me, Andrea. Please, you have to see me. I'm right here."

She placed her hand atop her mom's, but it passed right through. No! Frantically, she grasped in vain for her mom's arm, skirt, legs.

Finally, Andrea whirled to confront the Puritan girl, but she was gone.

She gazed up to question her mother.

But she was dead.

***

Her wrists were bound behind her back.

Miranda glanced down at herself. She was once again standing barefoot on a horse-drawn wagon beside the oak tree. A noose lay flaccidly around her neck. This time, she remained in her own clothing, and she was alone. No onlookers. No Camille.

"This isn't how it happened."

Miranda gagged as the noose tightened around her neck. A face appeared over her shoulder.

"Of course it isn't, witch, because this time I'm going to kill you and take your soul just like I've taken Camille's."

"Nathaniel. What have you done to her?"

"You should be more concerned about what I'm going to do to you, Ruth. Oh, and have you noticed how suddenly well versed I've become with modern English? I've had over three hundred years to learn it from all the tourists trespassing through my relocated home."

"I'm not Ruth Abbott."

"But you were and you murdered me, remember?"

"In self-defense when you tried to rape me."

"I offered you a chance to save your daughter's life."

"Where is she?"

Nathaniel spun her around and pointed across the road where Camille remained locked in the pillory. Beside it stood another. It was empty. *Reserved for me, no doubt.*

"Camille refused to move on to a new life after she was hanged," Nathaniel said.

Her conversation with Peter and Betsy came back to her.

"Camille is trapped here, in this time, in this place. No matter how we try to convince her to move on, she cannot bring herself to leave. She has been waiting all this time."

"For what?"

"For you."

"Without you," Nathaniel continued, "she was frightened and confused. I merely took advantage of her fear and now she is mine. Yet, I've always wondered why you were allowed to live again while I remained trapped here."

"Maybe because a monster like you doesn't deserve a new life."

At that, Nathaniel backhanded her across her face. "You were always too willful for your own good, Ruth. You never learned your place, but you will." He smiled as he leapt from the wagon and made his way toward the front of the cart. Reaching up, he retrieved the horsewhip from the bench. "Consider this a family reunion!"

Camille looked up at Miranda, face streaked with tears. Her words spilled out. "I just wanted to see you again. I never meant for this to happen. I am sorry."

"You have no reason to be, sweetie." Miranda flinched at the crack of the whip. Hooves beat against the dirt road. The floor moved beneath her feet. The noose tightened. "I love you, Cam—"

***

Frightened by the dream about her mother and the strange Puritan girl, Andrea took off in the middle of the night and drove home in record time. The living room light was on when she entered. Beside the front door, her mother's boots lay haphazardly on the floor beside unpacked luggage. A short stack of mail lay atop the coffee table. Otherwise, all seemed in order. Her mother was probably sound asleep, yet something felt wrong. For starters, the house was freezing.

Andrea made her way over to the thermostat and cranked up the heat before heading toward the steps. On her way up, she flipped the switch to turn on the upstairs hallway light—and collided with a pair of legs dangling in mid-air. Her heart slammed in her chest as she reeled back and lost her footing. With a yelp, she tumbled back down the steps and landed on her side.

Pushing hair out of her eyes, Andrea's mouth fell open at the sight of her mother levitating several feet above the stairs as if hanged by the neck. Her wrists were pressed together behind her back. Yet, there were no visible restraints. Drooping eyelids cast down a lifeless gaze from her tilted head.

"Oh, God, no!" Andrea bolted up the steps until she was almost at eye level with her mother. Her body rotated slowly at the end of an invisible rope. Andrea passed a hand over her mother's head. Nothing there. The skin around her neck was constricted and bruised. Andrea pressed her fingers against the side of her mother's throat. There was a pulse, albeit weak.

"Mom? Can you hear me? Look at me, please!"

There was no response. Andrea grabbed her mother's arms and tried to move her to no avail. She ran her hands through her hair as frustration drove her to tears. "What the fuck do I do now?" She leaned against her mother. "God, help me. Please don't take her away from me. Show me what I need to do… please!"

***

"There is nothing to do but wait, child. If your mother truly cares about you then once she is dead, her soul will come back here to be with you and then I will control you both… for eternity."

Keeping her head low and her eyes to the ground, Camille refused to meet her uncle's gaze. She did not understand this talk of "moving on" to a new life. Once you die, your soul travels to heaven or hell. Surely, this place was the latter. The devil had taken the form of Uncle Nathaniel and was punishing her and her mother. That was the only reasonable explanation.

Near the top of the dirt road to her right, a brilliant white light exploded into view. Camille winced against its brilliance. It glowed even through her eyelids. A warm breeze caressed her face and hands, carrying with it a sense of peace that somehow soothed her mounting fear.

"No," Nathaniel snarled. "I will not leave this place until I avenge myself upon these witches."

"Nathaniel Abbott," a voice beckoned from a distance. It was a young voice, unmistakable. "It is time to pay for your crimes."

Peter?

Camille opened her eyes. What she saw filled her with hope. As her vision adjusted to the light, blurred shadows sharpened into approaching silhouettes. She counted six. Behind them, the light vanished as quickly as it appeared. As the group closed in, familiar faces came into focus. All of them were from the village and all had been executed for witchcraft.

Sent to their deaths by Uncle Nathaniel.

Four of them surrounded him while Peter and Betsy hurried to the oak tree.

While Betsy embraced Camille's mother, Peter scaled the tree and crawled along the bottom branch. Pulling a knife from his belt, he sliced through the rope. Seconds later, Camille closed her eyes and prayed as her mother was lowered to the ground in Betsy's arms.

***

Her mother dropped into her arms, knocking Andrea off-balance and sending both women tumbling down the steps in a tangle of arms and legs.

Ignoring her own pain, Andrea rolled her mother over. "Mom, can you hear me? Please come back to me."

***

"She's alive."

Camille's knees buckled as she cried with joy. She wanted desperately to break free of her bonds and join Betsy at her mother's side.

By now, the other four had seized Nathaniel and pinned him against the wagon. Peter leapt from the tree and scooped up the rope as he joined them. "Ruth was correct, Nathaniel. You do not deserve a new life. Your soul has a different destiny."

"Leave me alone!" Nathaniel struggled, to no avail, as Peter slid the noose around his neck and tightened the knot.

Clutching the other end of the rope, Peter climbed into the wagon and looked around. Finding a gap between two of the sideboards, he threaded the rope through and tied it off just as another light appeared in the distance. Grim faces turned to watch as it grew into a circle that encompassed the entire width of the road. This time, however, it was dim and gray. Camille flinched at the unbridled hatred and fear that emanated from it.

Nathaniel's eyes widened. It seemed he felt it, too. "You deserved your fates. Filthy witches, all of you!" He looked from Camille to Ruth. "Just like them. You all consort with the devil."

Peter rounded the cart and stopped beside the horse, whip in hand. "Never met him, but I'm sure he'll enjoy your company."

"Wait!"

Camille turned her head to see her mother on her feet. With some assistance from Betsy, she approached the pillory and held out her hand. "Come to me, Camille."

"Mother, I... I cannot."

"Yes you can, sweetie."

"I am locked in here. It is my punishment. Uncle Nathaniel—"

"No longer has power over you. Come to me right now."

Camille set her jaw, imagined her hand in her mother's—and promptly fell to her knees as the pillory crumbled around her.

Her mother smiled. "That's my girl."

Camille picked herself up and ran into her mother's open arms. "I have waited so long for you."

"I know, I'm sorry. There's only one thing left to do now."

Everyone parted as Miranda faced Nathaniel. She balled her right hand into a fist. "Witch? In my time, the proper term is *bitch*." She accented her final word with a punch to his jaw.

With Camille in tow, she approached Peter and extended her hand. He turned over the horsewhip and backed away. After one last glance at Nathaniel, Miranda flipped her wrist. The whip cracked, piercing the still air. Startled, the horse reared up and charged.

Mother and daughter watched as Nathaniel was dragged past their feet in a cloud of dust. His enraged roar faded as horse and wagon vanished into the gray void.

"Mother, what is that?"

"Think of it as a doorway of sorts." Miranda put her arm around Peter's shoulder. "Thank you." She faced the others. "All of you."

"It was the least we could do," Betsy said. "Now, Camille can move on."

Camille shook her head. "I do not understand."

Once again, the white light appeared at the top of the road.

"This one's for us," Peter said. The others shuffled past and made their way up the road. Peter and Betsy looked at Camille expectantly.

"We need a few moments," Miranda said. "I'll send her along shortly."

Peter smiled and nodded. "We'll be waiting."

Seconds later, the portal faded. In its place, a lone figure stood for a moment before making his way toward them. As he approached, a look of awe crossed Camille's face. She took a tentative step forward and whispered, "Father." She looked at Miranda. "Mother, do you not recognize him?"

Miranda shook her head. She placed a hand on Camille's back. "I'll walk you to him."

As they drew near, Miranda found him instantly attractive. He was a few inches taller than she, with a slim build. He removed his capotain to reveal thick raven hair, unevenly trimmed and combed back, with only a single wavy lock dangling over his forehead. He was clean-shaven with wide, crystal blue eyes.

Miranda pegged his age at thirty-five, tops. *I could see myself married to that.*

He smiled at both women as they came to a stop in the middle of the road.

"Father, how can you be here?" Camille looked to Miranda. "Or is this some trick of the devil?"

"It's definitely me," he said as he opened his arms to her. "I'll explain everything very soon, Camille." He kissed her on the cheek as they embraced.

Camille held onto him as if for dear life. "I never thought I would see you again."

"Impossible. There's always an again."

Camille pulled back. "What do you mean?"

He looked up at Miranda. "When you were Ruth, I was Job. We were married for nearly twenty years. Camille was our only child."

"She has your eyes."

"And her mother's beauty, not to mention her stubbornness. You were both willful women who never knew your place in this society." He grinned. "And for that, I was never more grateful. You two are the only ones I miss from this life." He held up the capotain. "I certainly don't miss the wardrobe."

"Who are you now?"

He shrugged. "I'm sort of between lives. Until recently, I was an architect named Paul, just as you're now a teacher, Miranda."

"That's right."

"I still haven't decided what I want to do next, but before I go anywhere, I wanted to prepare Camille to move on. I only learned about her situation recently. I had no idea that she'd been trapped here for so long. Thank you for saving her. She's long overdue for a fresh start."

Camille looked at Miranda, brow furrowed in confusion. "You are not really my mother?"

"Oh, sweetie, of course I am. Here and now, in this place, but eventually our lives end when we've learned all that we need to, and then each of us begins again, born into a new life with new lessons to learn. Before that happens, there's something I keep trying to say to you, but I'm always interrupted."

"What?"

"I love you, Camille."

For the final time, mother and daughter held each other until both women broke down into tears. They were still trembling when Miranda pulled away. She cupped her hands around Camille's face.

"Now, it's time for you to start a new life. To leave this behind and see a new world through fresh eyes."

"I don't know that I can. I've waited so long for you."

"Don't be afraid. One way or another, we will be together again in the future. We'll be different people with different names, but our souls will be the same, and that will be what draws our paths to cross again, I promise. You and I are inseparable."

"How will I know it's you?"

"You'll feel it. Trust me."

Camille nodded reluctantly and took her father's outstretched hand.

"Right now, Miranda, your current daughter is in great distress," he warned. "She's with you now, but your body is injured and your breathing shallow. You don't have much time. You need to return to your life immediately. You've gone through so much to save Camille. Allow me to help you now. Until next time… Ruth."

***

Miranda opened her eyes and immediately began to gag. She rolled over onto her side and launched into a coughing fit.

"Mom!"

Hands touched her shoulder and arm. A face loomed above her, but tears clouded her vision. "Camille," she croaked.

"Camille? Who's that?"

"She's my… Andrea."

"Yeah, mom, I'm here."

Miranda inhaled sharply and closed her eyes. Her coughing subsided and she allowed herself to flop onto her back. "My daughter." She reached up.

Andrea took her hand and squeezed. "Last I checked. Take it easy, Mom. I'm calling an ambulance."

Miranda shook her head. "No. Don't need it."

"Mom, you were hanging by your neck above the steps."

"I'll be fine. Just give me a few minutes. I think he healed me."

"Who?"

"Job or Paul or whoever he was."

"I don't know what you're talking about."

"It's a long story. Just help me off the floor."

***

Andrea anxiously paced the living room while her mother sat on the end of the sofa, head resting in her hand.

"You're going to wear out the carpet."

With a sigh, Andrea took a seat at the opposite end of the sofa. "Are you sure I shouldn't call an ambulance?"

"I said I'm fine. No pain. I can breathe. It's all good."

Andrea leaned close. "The marks on your neck are gone. That's amazing. Are you going to tell me what happened?"

"So, how was your weekend?"

Andrea hesitated. "I was hoping you wouldn't ask."

Miranda lifted her head. "Did Wendy appear to you?"

"She did that, and other things."

"Tell. Me."

"Now doesn't seem to be a good time."

"Tell... me."

Her stomach quivering, Andrea launched into the events beginning with her visit from Ross and ending with her adventure at Stewart Lake. Albeit, she neglected to mention the attack on campus, running naked through the woods, and the damage to her telescope case.

Fifteen minutes later, her mother stared at her blankly as she finished her tale. "Life was so much simpler in 1692."

Andrea frowned. "What?"

"Never mind. You let Wendy possess you and put your life in danger. Didn't I warn you about that?"

"I swear, I meant to call you for advice as soon as Ross appeared, but then I had to run to Wendy's memorial, and… and then… well, let's just say things happened so fast after that. She came to me and asked me for help and I thought I could deal with it on my own, but it got out of control. You were right and I'm sorry, okay? When it was over, I left messages on your cell phone and the house phone, but I felt something was wrong. Then I had a nightmare about you, so I rushed home."

Miranda leaned forward. "That man could've killed you in the woods and then what? I get a call that they pulled your body from the bottom of the lake?"

"Wendy wouldn't have let that happen, and she didn't. I mean, here I am, right? A few cuts and bruises, but I'm in one piece. What about you? I come home to find you hanging by your neck by some… ghost rope. Care to explain that?"

Her mother took a deep breath… and burst out laughing. She slouched back into the sofa and cackled uncontrollably.

"Mom, are you sure you're all right?"

Miranda gave a desultory wave as she tried to regain her composure—and failed. Her entire body shook until she doubled over, clutching her sides.

"You're freaking me out, Mom."

Finally, Miranda forced her breathing into a calm rhythm and wiped the tears from her face. She looked at Andrea and shook her head. "Ghost rope? Ghost rope. You are too funny." She patted the cushion beside her. "Come here."

Andrea shook her head.

Miranda chuckled. "Nothing's going to happen. Just come here."

Cautiously, Andrea slid across the sofa and into Miranda's arms. "I love you… Drea."

"I love you, too, but I'm scared out of my mind. The police are probably going to question me again, and then—oh, God—the hospital bills, and I can just imagine what Dad's going to say when he finds out, not to mention—"

"Hush. We'll get through it, I promise, after we get some sleep." Miranda kissed her on the cheek and pressed her forehead against Andrea's. "You realize of course that you're now officially mini-me."

"Oh, no," Andrea groaned. "Can't we just say like mother, like daughter?"

"That seems to be true no matter what, where," her mother smiled, "or when."

Praise for "Freedom's Blood"

"I loved the vampire character in this novella. He was real. [He] has depth, both dark and a hint of light about him… Not the romantic 'Twilight' version of a vampire… He has such a personality and sharp wit yet with a hint of human in him still."

- Beryl Snyder on Goodreads

"Freedom's Blood was entertaining and at times amusing."

- Sue Frey

"A triumph of a story putting a delightful spin on vampire myths. Witticism from the main character keeps the reader engaged to find out where he will go or what will happen next. I feel I want to pluck this character out of the story and journey with him as long as I'm not his next entrée. A sequel to this vampire is a must. Steven Wilson can add me as a fan of his work."

– Dawn Sooy, author of *From the Darkness*

By Steven Howell Wilson

The Arbiter Chronicles

Taken Liberty

Unfriendly Persuasion

Sacrifice Play

Peace Lord of the Red Planet

Freedom's Blood

By Steven Howell Wilson

Firebringer Press
Baltimore, Maryland

Freedom's Blood

By Steven Howell Wilson

Editing & Proofreading by Sandra Zier-Teitler and Paul Balzé

Cover and Book design by Ethan H. Wilson

Cover Art by Caio Cacau

ISBN: 978-1-948178-01-3

Published by Firebringer Press

I knew it was a bad idea all along. Well, all right, I should have known. I've been kicking myself for weeks now, because I should have known. I've successfully avoided this kind of situation for over 250 years.

Any idiot knows that a person contemplating suicide is, by definition, not in the best frame of mind; but I really believed the kid when he said he wanted to die. He was going to get what he wanted out of the deal, and I was going to get what I needed. Isn't that what makes a fair contract?

Perhaps I should back up a bit and give you the particulars. To understand the quandary I got into, and how I got into it, you first have to understand what I am.

I am a vampire. That's right – vampire. Blood-sucking. Undead. Turn into a bat and everything. Perhaps you expect a disclaimer about how I actually can walk in sunlight (can't touch the stuff) or how I'm not actually supernatural but just maladjusted and blood-loving. Nope. Drink it. Gotta have it.

Live forever as long as I do – well, if I stay away from wooden stakes and get back to my coffin by curfew. I am not myth. The blonde kid on TV that makes vampires disappear in a cloud of ash? She's your myth. Never met the human who was my equal. Rarely have I seen one of my kind get staked. Certainly not while they were awake and could do something to prevent it!

Most of what you've heard is true. Garlic affects me the way tear gas does you. A stake through the heart will kill me. Won't do you any good either. Crucifixes? Uh uh. Yes, they've tended to scare our kind over the centuries, because those who wear them have tended to try to kill us over the centuries. I'm too intelligent a beast to say that all those who worship at the sign of the cross are murderous bigots, but I can see why less intelligent beasts could draw that conclusion. There's just so much evidence.

Holy water? Look, be realistic. My body chemistry is different from yours. Some things that hurt me don't hurt you and vice versa. Superstition doesn't enter into it. It's all about science. Your dog doesn't get sick from eating chocolate because Hershey was a cat person, he gets sick because the stimulant it contains cannot be quickly processed by his digestive system, and builds up to a toxic level in his blood. Your system processes theobromine, the stimulant, quickly, and so you do not get sick from eating chocolate. Your immunity and his vulnerability exist no matter what religious ceremonies are performed over the chocolate.

So why would a little glass of water that was muttered over by a sexually frustrated cleric give me gas? If water doesn't hurt me, the ritual won't change the fact.

And water doesn't hurt me. In fact, I can walk on it – or under it – with no troubles. I suspect that, at some point during the Spanish Inquisition days, one of their bright boys took it upon himself to put some corrosive agent or other into holy water, and happened to fling it in the face of a vampire who (surprise!) felt pain.

Oh, and if my ability to walk on water causes you to feel the need to worship me, I have no objection; but a shrine in your home would have little meaning for me. If you're so moved, send ten per cent of your pre-tax earnings to me care of this publisher, and I will transfer to you, faithfully each night, intangible religious benefits. I further promise you that, should I ever meet any being approaching omnipotence, I will put in a good word for you with Him. Or Her. Or It.

Fair deal? No pressure. Think about it. I have lots of time.

Now that you're clear on what a vampire is, you'll of course want to know how I became one. It was the usual way: I was bitten by another vampire and I tasted his blood – my blood in his veins, to be precise. It happened like this...

Oh, before I go further, I would like to make it clear that this is my story, and will not now devolve into a history of the person – creature – who sired me.

The creature who made me a vampire is not interesting, continental or a good model for a hair gel commercial. In fact, he was an accountant with bad breath. And yes, halitosis is offensive, even to vampires. Especially to us, as what is more distasteful than one who plies a trade but does not keep his tools of that trade well maintained? Even an unwilling victim deserves some consideration, don't you think?

Would you want to be bitten by fangs caked with traces of many blood types – some horribly diseased! – which had little bits of venous tissue lodged between them? I should say you would not!

An odious creature. I burned him three days later because it was cold. Oh, vampires

don't get cold you say? And you may be right. But I'll never tell.

I was born in the town of Harper's Ferry, the colony of Maryland, in 1743. At sixteen, I had been apprenticed to a smith for three years. Interesting work, smithing. Its best aspect for a young man is that he gets to play with fire a lot. Its worst is that he tends to burn himself in rather embarrassing places. I had not chosen it. My father had. He wanted me to have a trade. I, on the other hand, wanted me to have a large manor house, a sizeable fortune, and a baker's dozen buxom serving girls. The prospect of taking over for old man Weber when he became too infirm to lift his hammer did not seem likely to carry me to that manor house. Nor did the frequent beatings I received – the result of my habit of reading whenever my master was not looking.

I decided to run away. Somewhere. I wasn't sure where. Baltimore sounded as though it might have promise. Or Philadelphia. I was somewhat educated – Mother was a preacher's daughter – and might find work in a printer's shop, or with a trading company, and eventually go into business. That was the path to wealth!

So I didn't go home that night. It was an all or nothing decision. If I hesitated – stayed out for while, went a little ways – then turned around and went

home late, the whipping would be unendurable. So, to spare my posterior, I spent the evening seeking the best method of transit out of Harper's Ferry. I'd brought a little money – a few coins. I thought to bribe the driver of some horse cart or coach to take me as far as Frederick or Hagerstown.

After three very cold hours, wandering High Street in the rain, ducking into shadow often, lest my father be looking for me, I saw a coach pull up at the Tavern. Here was my chance. I waited in the shadow of a stone-walled embankment while the driver unloaded the baggage of the only passenger – an over-dressed Englishman. Once the fop was within and annoying the innkeeper, and the driver was checking the tack on his horse, I approached, coins in my hand.

The reception was not a warm one. The driver was not interested in transacting business. Judging by the names he called me, I can only gather he thought I was a beggar, an orphan, who intended to slit his throat when we were beyond the meager lights of the town. I'm sure I looked quite ragged, after hours in the rain. Perhaps he had had bad experiences with young travelers in the past. I don't know. All I know was that he pulled away, leaving me sitting in the street, blood trickling from my lip where he'd cuffed me, my proffered coins cast to the cobblestones about me.

Behind me, there was a gentle ahem. I turned. It was the Englishman. He observed that I was bleeding. That, I suppose, should have been a dead giveaway; but I was young and naive to the ways of the Vampir. He expressed regret at my treatment at the hands of the driver, and asked if I needed a place to stay. Naive? Very naive. I agreed.

He bought me rum. Looking back, I'm befuddled by that. At the time, I was befuddled by the rum itself. Now I am befuddled by the purchase of it. Vampires drink blood. That is our sustenance. Any impurity in it is, well, a distraction. If you think liquor might improve the flavor, think of drinking your evening glass of warm milk with sawdust stirred in. It probably wouldn't hurt you, but you wouldn't enjoy it.

So why did he buy me rum? I can only conclude that he enjoyed the hunt. Setting the scene. Getting the young victim drunk, and, essentially, seducing him. Possibly even getting him to ask for the pleasure of the bite. In short, the bastard liked to play with his food.

I must have amused him, because he let me live... after a fashion. When he was done with me – the perverse sod had dragged me up the hill and into the cemetery that overlooks much of the town – he leaned me against a tombstone. I was drunk, weak from anemia. My head lolled stupidly on my shoulders, and I wondered why it was so unseasonably cold on a night in April.

"What do you want?" he asked me curiously.

I wasn't sure what he meant. I wanted to be warmer. I wanted to go to sleep. I wanted very much to vomit and be done with it. But... his question seemed to have a much weightier feel to it than to simply ask me the desires of the moment. So I told him, "I want an estate, a sizeable fortune, and a baker's dozen buxom serving girls."

He studied me, my blood still smeared on his lips. "I very much think you might get them," he said, At the time, I thought he meant he was going to give

them to me. It took me a while to realize that what he meant was that he expected me to make myself wealthy. Perhaps that is why he granted me eternal life on this plane. He hoped that I, out of gratitude for the gift, would quarter him in my estate, spend my fortune on him, and toss him whichever of the wenches I wasn't using on a given evening.

If that was his plan, he did not figure into it my natural impatience. I remained with him three days: long enough to learn that he was a factotum – an accountant, in today's words. He had been an accountant, at any rate. Now he was a freelance bloodsucker. Normally, I object to the term "parasite" being applied to one of my kind. Parasites depend on their host's continued life, but offer them no assistance in extending that life. We are predators. We kill. But the creature who sired me was a parasite. He had nothing to offer anyone. Being a vampire had not made him that way. He was naturally that way.

I burned him three days later, in a field, by a nice little stream just outside what is now Towson.

* * *

I arrived in Baltimore later that same day, ravenously hungry. I drank a bum. Killed him, of course. That was what my sire had done with his victims, myself excepted. I was merely continuing as he had taught me. Besides, the bum was near death anyway. He'd polluted his body to the point that his liver was about to fail. It was one of the worst meals of my life, to that point and to this day. Still, I was sated, and had time to be choosy with my next meal.

On the evening of my second solo kill, I went where most of the city went for food – to the market. Lexington Market, in this case. Only I had no interest in the fresh fruits and vegetables arriving by wagon from remote farms. The meats caught my eye, but then my nose assessed them, and I was shocked by my revulsion. They were dead. Since my change, I could no longer bring myself to consider dead flesh. It stank to me as spoiled food would to you.

In the wee hours of the morning, however, the market was stocked to the gills with my food – people. The farmers arrived hours before dawn with their produce, readying themselves for morning and the arrival of customers. Most of them weren't appetizing. Old. Tough. Dirt under their nails. Scented with manure. (The presentation of the meal matters for my kind too.)

Is it too trite that I selected that staple of male humor, a farmer's daughter? Fresh. Young. Clean. About sixteen. Her eyes were clear and green like spring maple leaves, and her teeth had not had time to go bad. Beneath her simple, home-crafted dress, newly erupted breasts pushed at their constraining fabric, and firm buttocks moved seductively with each step she took.

I was hungry now on two counts.

I waited in the shadows across Eutaw Street until the male members of her family moved away. Fools. I would never have left her alone in the city. I approached, said hello.

She smiled at me, a flirtatious but honest smile. "Don't you have work to do for your father?" she asked, assuming I was from one of the other farm families. Certainly, I was still dressed as a laborer.

"I'm... not with my father," I said.

She appraised me. "You're a little young to be here alone. Your master, then."

"I'm not here to work," I said. "I'm hungry."

"You look a little thin," she admitted. Then she frowned, and seemed to be considering her options. "The market's not open for a few hours, but I could – " She reached for an apple.

"No," I said. "I – I wanted something more than that."

"I'd like to help," she said skeptically, "but you don't look like you have any money."

"I have something valuable to trade. I could show you."

"Well – "

"Only I don't want to show you here. Someone might see. Let's go over there."

I pointed to a dark corner some yards away.

Her face became suspicious. "You've stolen something, haven't you?"

"No, honestly, I've not. Just come over here."

"Well – "

"Please?"

I suppose I looked young, innocent and harmless enough that she followed me. Do I flatter myself to say that perhaps I also looked attractive enough, despite my scruffy condition, to have lured a pretty girl to a dark corner? Perhaps. Anyway, she followed me.

"Well?" she demanded, "What is it you have?"

"I told you I was hungry," I said simply, and fell upon her. She yelped when I tore her dress to the waist, exposing the breasts I'd admired beneath. I was not disappointed when they came into view, but I had a more immediate goal than the admiration of her body.

When she saw my fangs, she screamed at the top of her lungs. I was too crazed with blood lust to care. I lowered my head, pierced the area around one nipple with my teeth, and nursed at her breast. She struggle beneath me, kicking and clawing. At first, this disconcerted me. I was never a boy given to cruelty.

As her blood flowed warm and soothing into me, however, her violent attentions became welcome. The pain of her nails raking my shoulders and arms, the heat of her body as it bucked beneath mine, quickened my pulse and drove the excitement of conquest to new heights.

It was then that I learned my first, painful lesson about being a vampire. While I was intent on my gratification, the girl's father and brothers had returned. Bad enough I was killing their daughter and sister, but the state of her clothing made them believe I was committing an even graver offense. (Humans. I don't get them.)

They leapt upon me, shrieking more loudly than the girl. I heard other voices expressing concern and interest. A mob would certainly form. I could smell that the girl had died as their fists drove into me. Fools again. They had worried more over revenge than the safety of their own.

I had to escape before the situation became unmanageable. I drank my fill of the youngest brother. The other two I simply killed quickly as obstacles. I fled, hearing the screams and cries of horror as the drained bodies were discovered. They followed me through the cold, night air as I ran through the shadows of Pratt Street. They echoed in my mind as, engorged, I crawled beneath a dock at the harbor and fell asleep.

* * *

When I awoke, I was appalled – appalled at my own actions and my own stupidity. I was not old enough to have gone on benders while still human. I didn't realize at the time that the sensation was very like that of a man awakening with a terrible hangover, and realizing that he'd bedded his host's ugly wife in the back room at a party the night before.

I realized quickly that I'd made all the worst mistakes of the vampire on that one kill. I'd left evidence. I'd allowed myself to be discovered. I'd let my passions govern me, drunk on the flavor of my victim's fear, and on her sexual attractiveness. I'd made no attempt to control the situation, or the girl's responses to it. I knew that a vampire possessed a hypnotic gaze which silences, but I'd gotten too caught up in the moment to use it. Now, no doubt, there would be constables and angry mobs out searching for a monster.

Stupid.

I credit myself that I realized my mistakes as quickly as I did. It's because I learn from experience that I've lived to have so much of it. I did not repeat those mistakes with another victim.

It was not my stupidity, however, that troubled me most that clear evening as I wandered beneath the stars and beside the waters of the Chesapeake. No, what troubled me most was that I had taken a young and innocent life. With the bum, I had performed an act of charity, ending a miserable life which was of no value to its owner or anyone else. With the girl, I had murdered. Then I had, in my madness, killed three poor, dumb souls who had only sought justice.

I could have borne this, but for the beliefs already ingrained within me. Beliefs which have deepened as, over the centuries, I have furthered my studies. I mentioned earlier that I was a reader, and a voracious one. No amount of physical pain could stop me from carrying a book everywhere I went, and opening it whenever no one required my attention.

At sixteen, I had read all of the Greek philosophers. I had read Locke and Rousseau. I held a firm conviction that Man was a free creature, with a divinely granted right to pursue happiness and produce wealth, free of molestation or interference by others. Unprovoked violence, theft and tyranny were therefore wrong. I could not escape the conclusion that imbibing the blood of a man, woman or child – taking his or her property – was... wrong.

At that time in history, the greatest villain we knew in America was King George III. I realized that I had, unwillingly, been made kin to this villain. Most, if not all rulers are like unto vampires. They need your life's blood in order to enhance their own situation, and consider themselves perfectly justified in taking it, based on their need. If King George's oppressive taxation of the Colonies was wrong, then what I had done to that innocent child was equally so.

And so I could not rationalize away murder, and so it was in Baltimore that I established for myself a firm code of behavior, which I have since never broken.

Vampires must kill to live, and so I had to diverge from my philosophical forbears. I had to become a moral authority unto myself, assuming the power of life and death.

Could I feed without ever killing? Not really. There are three possible outcomes for a vampire's victim. The first is death. The second is one-time or limited use of the subject, followed by a period of rest and eventual recovery. The third is conversion of the subject to vampirism himself. Option one can be distasteful. Option two is dangerous, as living victims can betray you.

Option three is, in my opinion, highly unethical. I have never sired another vampire, never allowed a subject to taste of my blood. Why? Because vampirism confers a great deal of power. We can become invisible. We can transform into bats, wolves, and mists. We're very hard to kill. Worst, we can enslave the will of a free person. I have never met another in whom I would entrust such power.

Unable to sustain himself, therefore, on living victims, a vampire has no choice but to occasionally kill. The only alternative is starvation. So I kill.

I take responsibility for my own actions. I do not claim I should be forgiven my killings because a kind of insanity (hunger) seizes me and makes me kill. If I happen to eat your brother, I do not fault you if you try to stake me. I'll just try like hell to prevent you doing so, and I'll probably arrange a cash settlement to compensate you for your loss. Two centuries of dabbling in the market have left me filthy rich.

Do I think I can just eat people and then pay their relatives, as if the world was my restaurant? No, I don't. But you'd be amazed how many family members would happily accept going rate for a dinner entree in exchange for the life of a loved one. I've even had requests...

I do not feed off the innocent, or anyone with dependents or loved ones of any kind. I kill only those who are better off dead, are dying anyway, or who have forfeited their right to live.

The dying and better off dead include the failing elderly and long-infirm. A steady diet of these, however, leaves one listless. They have been close to death for so long, drinking of them is close to drinking the blood of a corpse. Dangerous indeed! A healthy diet for my kind requires the regular consumption of blood from the healthy and vital... or the recently so.

A character in a Monty Python sketch once lamented that "there simply aren't enough accidents." From my point of view, however, the number is sufficient. In America, I keep a fire and police scanner with me always. When it notifies me of a fatal or potentially fatal accident, I quickly travel to the scene or the destination hospital.

These feedings leave no evidence, as there are frequently open wounds I may use, rather than puncturing flesh. The victims, when conscious, do not object to my ministrations. My hypnotic ability relieves some of the pain, and death, obviously, shortens its duration.

The final category of moral killings I allow myself can be satisfying. Oh, get that look off your face! Can't a man enjoy his food? I refer, of course, to revenge killings. Perhaps I should call them equity killings. These are people who have forfeited their right to live by committing murder. (I am well aware that I myself am in that last category.) Civil Society dictates that all thefts should be punished by making the thief render restitution. If the thief steals someone's life, well, what does he have to give in return but his own?

I make it a point to follow murder cases, often conducting my own investigation. I investigate murders to learn two things: One, the identity of the murderer and two, the desires of the victim's family. If the family does not wish the death of the guilty party, I go about my business. If they do, and the murderer is not executed, I act.

Finally, you ask, why do I not eat politicians? For the same reason you do not eat dog food. If you do eat dog food, I apologize, and send me your contact info via this publisher. You'd make a wonderful politician-eating vampire, and we need one.

* * *

I began this missive by telling you I was in a moral quandary. Here it is: I'd drained a victim to the point of no return – he wasn't going to live, no matter who intervened, but he wasn't dead yet. He'd asked to die, and now he'd changed his mind. Tough luck, you say? There's nothing I can do for him, you say? Ah, but there was something I could do for him, and he knew exactly what it was.

I didn't want to do it. Not on a bet.

* * *

It was early August, and I was in San Diego. I'd been having a very nice time. I'd come early to see the sights, before attending the Cato Institute's summer seminar. By design, I'd missed their events for the last few years; but this year, American libertarians seemed to have recovered from most of their September 11th-

inspired tendency to encourage war. I was glad, for I really wanted to be among thinking people again.

I'd spent the early dusk hours in an Irish pub in the Gas Lamp district, flirting with an outspoken bartender from Boston and sipping Guinness. No, I never drink wine; but Guinness is something you never outgrow, even when you don't grow any longer. It doesn't affect me at all, and the taste is totally altered by my condition. I still just like the experience of sipping the odd Guinness in the odd Irish pub.

As I attempted to make my case to this opinionated young woman, who simply would not believe that Killian's Irish Red was, in fact, brewed in Colorado, a bulletin about a traffic accident came on the omnipresent television. It was nearly ten, and the traffic reports long over, but it seemed that this accident involved enough vehicles that it had actually closed Pacific Highway going northbound. Six people were dead, and medevac helicopters were rushing patients from the scene.

I suddenly remembered I was hungry. As the local news commentator began to interview a spokesman for the police about how undemocratic it was that drivers of SUVs tended to survive more such accidents than drivers of economy cars, I tapped the dummy pager I always wear.

"I have a call," I told my Celtic sparring partner. "Gotta run."

"Is it about that accident?" she asked. "You a doctor?"

I smiled. "Among other things." I tipped her entirely too much, slipped onto the street and into a dark corner, and flew. Literally. You cover a lot of ground as a bat.

In fact, I hadn't lied to the barkeep. I am a doctor. Studied at the Sorbonne, in the late 1890s. I've kept up my knowledge via books and medical journals. I'm not licensed to practice anywhere. How could I be? Licensing requires that someone know who and where I am.

But being a physician in fact, if not by law, does allow me to assess the condition of a subject, to know when death is imminent, and, in many cases, to ease the suffering of those I'm dealing with. (Occasionally, I've increased the suffering, but only occasionally. Perhaps you could force yourself to be impartial and gentle with, for instance, a mother who murdered her children in order to catch a husband. I am not so saintly.)

The scene of the accident was, as expected, grisly. I did not count the vehicles involved, as such details don't help me in any way. Nor do they help most people, other than to indicate magnitude of damage, and give an idea of how long it will take for the roadway to be cleared. Unless a family member is involved, or you need to travel that particular road, I have no idea why you would want to read about or see footage of a traffic collision. Or any calamity with an airplane, train, or other conveyance. If you are not directly affected, or able to use the story of the occurrence to increase your own personal safety, I do not see why you would want to know.

Perhaps I am hard-hearted. Strike "perhaps." I know I am. But I see no virtue in reviewing and sharing the pain of people you don't even know. It is a false compassion you feel, if your feelings go anything beyond "that's too bad, I hate to see that happen to

anyone," or "I would hate for that to happen to myself or my loved ones." The media works very hard to convince us that these events do affect us, and that we should feel the same loss that the victim's old mum does. It's good for their business, but it's very bad for our peace of mind. It often damages our ability to set our own priorities and attend to the needs of those to whom we do owe our compassion.

By the time I arrived, a seventh patient had died, thus becoming useless to me. Most of the more critical cases had been transported to the hospital already. One helicopter was preparing to take off, just then. After a quick scan of the other injured, all but two of whom were standing on their own power, I decided I would accompany the patient in the 'copter. Its blades were already spinning. A problem for me. A bat cannot easily approach a grounded helicopter when its blades are generating air currents. A bat doesn't weigh enough to resist. A mist would blow right away. A dog would attract too much attention. I was forced to assume my own form – for a moment. Once I was at the 'copter, I misted myself and floated in. One young paramedic did see me, out of the corner of her eye. I made sure I was not there for her second look. My ghostly appearance and disappearance frightened her. I heard her pulse race. She didn't stop working on her patient, however, and I didn't hear her mention it to her cohorts. People don't like to discuss any sign that they are hallucinating. That is a powerful weapon in my arsenal.

As a bat, I snuggled beneath an equipment bag at the rear of the cabin. I watched. The victim being transported was an adult male. He looked to be in

his mid-forties. I could tell by the sound of his chest cavity that he had sustained severe internal injuries. My hearing may just be a better diagnostic tool than ultrasound or MRI. If my people ever do become accepted in human society, I intend to make another fortune working as a diagnostician. I'll merely have to solve the problem of how to make my enhanced senses switch on without alarming my patients. It takes the smell of fresh blood to do it. This poor man had much fresh blood on him and coming out of him.

He wasn't going to live. Not even an hour was left to him.

I felt hunger pangs. They weren't in my stomach – ours never are. Hunger, for us, is a chill in the blood. Our skin is always cold. Folktale informs you of that fact, doesn't it? Still, our body temperature does vary. It's just always colder than yours... while you're living. When we have fed, the warm blood warms us throughout. Our system operates at peak efficiency, digesting and recirculating. We don't feel hunger again until we have processed what we've taken in, and our body temperature lowers again. No fuel to keep the furnace going.

The paramedic stayed with him, checking vital signs, attempting to keep him stable until they arrived at the hospital. There was no way I could feed without being seen. Some vampires would have leapt at the chance to wreak havoc at this juncture. I could have resumed human form, likely causing the girl before me to urinate in terror. I could have feasted on the dying man, then on her, then on the pilot. I could have sent the 'copter on a downward plunge, with a terrific explosion to destroy all of the evidence of my visit. I could have easily escaped all of this unharmed.

I was not about to do it. These people had done nothing to deserve such a fate. Even at my hungriest, I had not broken the code I'd developed in Baltimore. So, hunger or no hunger, I had to wait until we landed, and I had a better opening. I crept quietly along the floor to the base of the patient's stretcher, which would stay with him all the way into an operating room at the ER. Nestled under the vinyl flange of its cushion, I pulled my bat's wing over my head and took a nap.

* * *

The restrained jolt of the stretcher being lowered to the ground awakened me. Tuning out the chatter as the patient's condition was recited to a physician, I listened for his vital signs myself. They were ebbing quickly. He might not live to reach an operating table, and my waiting would be for naught. Still, I had no choice but to ride this out. If he died too quickly, well, it was a hospital. Food could not be far away.

They never even operated. Time of death was called immediately upon examination, and the body was left in a darkened cubicle for pickup. There were many other patients from the same accident to be seen. The ER staff did not waste time.

Fortunately for me, they did miscall the time of death. Human doctors often do. That's not to say that they so often abandon patients who could be saved. I merely mean that the actual death – the moment when the blood becomes useless to me – often comes seconds or minutes after they have declared it to be passed. Just as often, they will attempt to save a patient who has passed that threshold already.

In this case, I was left in a darkened room with a potential corpse. It was dinner time. I shifted to my human form. No one from the hospital would come in here until the chaos without had quieted. The victim's family would be some time arriving. The roads were still backed up from the accident.

I hadn't counted on the morbid tendencies of some teenagers.

The boy didn't burst in on me. He was very quiet, actually. He slowly opened the door, and gave his eyes a few seconds to adjust to the dark. I must have been distracted. I could have shifted to a less visible form in the blink of an eye, but I didn't. I didn't notice he was there until he'd seen me.

And he saw me. Blood on my chin and all.

"Oh my god," he murmured vaguely, something akin to surprise – but less intense – behind his eyes.

Now what? I wondered. Would he bolt from the room, announce my presence to all and sundry? I could escape easily enough. The boy's claims would be dismissed as the result of his injury. He had a bandage on his forehead, so I know he'd been injured. A head wound was the perfect type, too, but... dammit! I'd been sloppy.

Still, an expedient exit was best. I prepared to transform, tuning out, as I did, whatever potential inanities would utter forth from his lips, should he recover his voice. I catalogued them all for myself, inside a second:

"You're a vampire!"

or,

"Get away from me!"

or,

"Cool!"

or,

"Sorry, I didn't know this room was taken."

or,

"Help!"

Most likely, it would be the last. One of the disadvantages of a long life is that you develop a tendency to predict – with frightening accuracy – how the average person will react in any given situation. Another disadvantage is that, when your prediction is wrong, it tends to break your concentration and totally throw you off your game.

I hadn't expected him to say it, hadn't included it in my list of responses. I, therefore, did not tune it out. When he said it, I hesitated... and was lost.

"Did you kill him?"

He asked it quietly, without accusation. There was curiosity only in his tone. A practical person might have fled, taking advantage of the extra time he gave me by not shrieking for help right away. I have never been a practical person, nor ever wanted to be one. I confess that I place ethical and philosophical issues ahead of concerns of personal convenience, and, obviously, even safety.

He asked if I had killed. You no doubt realize by now that it is very important to me that I not be found guilty of ending a healthy life. Perhaps it did not matter what this one child thought, since he would never see me again. I still felt moved to explain that I had not, in fact, taken this innocent life. I had merely benefitted from its passing in much the same way an organ donor who had received the man's heart or liver might have.

"No," I told him quietly. "Internal injuries killed him. I just... went along for the ride."

"Oh," he said reasonably. Do not infer from that that he was reasonable by nature. He was not, nor had I any reason to believe, at that time, that he was. The evidence was all against it. The expression on his ordinary face was bewildered, perhaps a little vacuous. He seemed to be so calm when encountered by a supernatural creature, not because he was brave or very rational. No, he seemed just not to care one way or another. He hadn't the sense to be afraid.

A wise man does not panic, knowing his cool head will benefit him when in danger more than will his adrenaline. A fool does not panic because he's just too stupid to be afraid. That is not bravery, though it is often so labeled. The sloppy dress, the unkempt hair, the poor elocution of this young specimen all led me to believe that he was probably a fool. I don't say that to be insulting. Most people are fools. I'm used to it, and observe it as readily as I do that a person is male or female.

He stared dumbly, hands thrust in pockets beneath his t-shirt. "So... you eat here a lot?"

"I prefer to dine at the scene of the accident. The meal is fresher."

"Can't you just, y'know, hit a nightclub, or something?"

"I could. I choose not to kill those who aren't dying already... unless they deserve it."

"Do you..." He looked around furtively. "Do you kill people... who ask for it?"

"Sometimes." I gestured to the corpse, wiping blood from my lips with a napkin. There's no excuse for poor table manners, even when it's an operating table. "Is he a friend of yours? Relative?"

The boy shook his head. "Nope."

"Why did you come in here, then?"

"I... wanted to visit him. I saw them bring him in. I just... wondered what happened. Felt sorry for him. I was in the same accident."

"You and a great many people. You're lucky to be alive."

"No I'm not," he muttered.

"What?"

"You... feed... on people who ask for it?"

"I said I did. Unless I think they'll change their minds later."

"I won't change my mind."

"What are you saying, exactly?"

"I want you to feed off me. I want you to kill me."

Now here was an intriguing potential solution to my problem. I had wondered what I was to do about his discovery of me. Killing him was certainly neater and cleaner than running away. Besides, I had been looking forward to the Cato Seminar. I didn't want to flee San Diego just now. If he meant what he said...

"That's an easy thing to say," I countered.

"No it isn't. Not really. But I mean it."

"Why?"

He looked uncomfortably at the corpse. "Personal reasons. I'd rather not get into it."

"I'm sorry," I said, "but if you want me to take such an action, I must know your reasons. I'm very serious about my commitment not to take life unless I'm morally justified in doing so."

"Let's just say that I don't like my life very much," he said.

I can't say I trusted his judgment. On the other hand, he was young. He would make a good meal. I hadn't had really fresh blood lately. It was tempting. Still, I couldn't escape the feeling that, if I did kill him, it would be solely to protect my secret. Request or no request, I felt it boiled down to that. And it was my own stupid fault I'd been found out. It was my own stupid vanity that had made me wait around to explain myself to a mentally atrophied, teenaged stranger.

"I'm not hungry," I told him. "Go away."

He refused. Repeatedly.

He kept working at me. He worked at me a long time. After several minutes of haggling, he tried "take me with you, or I'll tell everyone I've seen you."

Weak. Very weak.

"Do you know my name?"

He shook his head.

"My address? Social Security number?"

"You have a Social Security number?"

"Twelve of them. You see, your threat is meaningless. You can tell these idiots that you saw me, but they most likely won't believe you. There aren't even any wounds on that body." I gestured at the table, then added, "Well, none that I put there."

"Someone might believe me. I'll take a lie detector test. And then they'll hunt you down and – "

"And I'll be in a different city, under a different name. I'm no fool. I've lived over two hundred years. Exposure only works on vampires who want to live in the same house for centuries, like that idiot on that soap opera."

"You mean *Dark Shadows*? My mom buys all the DVDs. You watch soap operas?"

"Of course, when they're about vampires."

He nodded, his face still empty. "Oh, right, how often do they make a show about Family?"

"Family?"

"Yeah. Y'know... Your own kind. I figured you people would – "

"Shut up. I hate that expression. 'Family,' to me means either the misguided belief of some homosexuals that all people who share their preference are spiritually connected, or a mediocre television program with Kristy McNichol. It does not describe the relationships between vampires. There are no relationships between vampires. Most of us can't stand each other."

This fact interested him briefly, but then he began whining and pleading anew. Eventually, I took him home with me. Now, before you say that it's not morally advisable to take a young person home, based on a claim made in a state of emotional distress, without the consent of his parents, I'll ask you to remember that I'm a vampire. I'm comfortable with things that might make you uncomfortable; and just because something makes you uncomfortable does not mean it's immoral.

When I took him home, my intent was to observe a cooling-off period. I'd tell him a few stories of death at the hands of a vampire. He'd see that it was neither erotic nor romantic. He'd go home to mommy. I'd find a nice, cold-blooded murderer and eat him.

But it was not to be. The road to hell, as they say...

Let me provide an illustration you may understand. Have you ever agreed to share a room, or even a bed, with a member of the gender – or a gender – to which you are attracted? Have you done so with the understanding that nothing of a sexual nature will happen? Convincing yourself as well as the other? Have you been able to keep the bargain?

Or perhaps I should compare the situation to having a piece of your favorite dessert sitting on the table in front of you. Let's make no mistake here, the boy was dessert. No drugs, no alcohol, no ravages of age to taint the meal. He was a triple-scoop hot fudge sundae, whipped cream, cherry and all, with brandy laced into the sauce and fresh, hot coffee steaming on the side. You can ignore it all you want... but if you let it just sit there, either someone else is going to eat it, or that beautiful thing is going to melt into a ruinous mass all over the tabletop.

Are you beginning to understand? In the end, I could not resist for long. After just twenty hours with him in my home, I had to taste him. I was not disappointed. The blood was delicious. I didn't take a lot. I've learned not to gorge, over the years. When I was done, I let him sleep it off for most of a day, after I had convinced him to eat a hearty meal. His body needed to replace all that blood, after all. He resisted, saying he was just going to die soon anyway. I managed to convince him that death, if it was soon to come, would be far easier if he kept up his strength.

Those analogies being made, let me clarify one point. I felt no sexual attachment to this particular meal. I know much is made in popular literature of

the erotic nature of vampirism. Women are described as having (or hinted to have had, in "cleaner" works) orgasms while being drained. The feeling of the victim toward the predator is compared to the all-consuming lust we feel for the dominator or dominatrix, if we are of that nature. But let's be realistic, shall we? Do you have sexual feelings for food? Never mind. I don't wish to know about it if you do. I think you see my point, however. And certainly, the food doesn't have sexual feelings for you. Can you imagine a cow or chicken, masturbating frantically to the thought of becoming a frozen sandwich patty? Ludicrous!

And it is equally ludicrous to suppose – putting aside the small number of deranged fetishists one might expect in any population – that any sexual feeling exists in the interaction between vampire and prey.

In my case, particularly, there would have been little chance of such feelings. As I have said already, my meals consisted of hardened criminals, terminally ill patients, victims of trauma and the mentally ill. My tastes might be very different from yours, but I assure you I do have taste. I will not say that I disapprove of sexual relations between males, nor that I have never entertained the thought of engaging in them; but I will say that my young victim, in this case, did nothing for me. Except to nourish me, of course.

When he awoke, the boy seemed none the worse for having provided me dinner from his own blood. Of course, he'd slept sixteen hours, and forced me – for the first time in decades – to visit a grocery store. Still, he seemed a normal, healthy, American teen.

But he still wanted to die. I pressed him at length to give me some reason for his self-destructive urge. Had a girl broken his heart? Was he not doing well in school? Did his peers treat him poorly? All of these he denied. He simply stated, over and over again, that he wished to end it all for "personal reasons."

I must admit I grew impatient – both with his moodiness and his recalcitrance. I decided anyone who moaned that much had to be miserable, and it was an act of charity to kill him. Besides, I had already taken first blood, if you'll pardon the expression. I'd drunk of him once. I could end it all in one session. Or I could stretch it out a few days – make the meal last. In any event, he would be an easy kill. I could have eaten two of him in a night.

I would do it, I told him.

And, being the liberal sort I am, I asked him how he wished to die. All at once? Over days? He thought for an hour, while he surfed the Internet. (He was amazed that a vampire would go on the Internet. Of course he would, I explained. He wants to prowl, and wants to keep up with the world. Being alienated, he wants to have the control over his information intake that the Internet allows. Besides, it can be great fun to go in a chat room and tell someone you're a vampire, prowling for your next meal...)

Having thought, he announced that he would like to die over the course of a few sessions. That should have forewarned me. No one who really wants to die wants to do so slowly. We began that night. I drained two pints or so from him. I told him I would drink from him again within a day, thus not allowing all of his blood to replace itself.

Two days later, having passed the point of no return, he threw a curve at me.

Point of no return, you ask? There comes a time when you've drained the victim too much, even if you're careful. His blood is now poisoned, and he's going to die. It's sort of like a blood cancer. The tainted cells are too many to be replaced.

The curve he threw? He announced it just after I'd fed one night, speaking slowly, quietly, as he was weakening now.

"I want to be one."

"One what?"

"One of what you are. A vampire."

I hesitated, not sure how to respond.

"You can do that, can't you?" he prompted.

What was I to say? Of course I could do it; but, for the reasons I elaborated earlier in this narrative, I would not do it. I started to tell him this –

"Of course you can do it," he said as I started to speak. His voice took on an edge. "And don't try to bullshit me about it, either. I know what you guys can do."

I began to wonder if this had been his intent all along – to convince me that he was a willing and disposable victim, then demand to be given the life eternal that I could bestow. Did he know what an uncomfortable position this put me in, ethically? Did he know what refusal would mean for me? How could he?

I trust you can conclude the quandary in which this left me, but I shall be tedious and state it outright. There are, no doubt, a fair share of idiots among my prospective readers. I want their money as much as I want... yours.

Fact: he was going to die. All right, perhaps not fact, but very probable supposition. Short of some miracle of medicine – I knew of no cure and I was the best doctor I'd ever met – he was too weak to go on. His blood was too poisoned. I doubted he would last the night. Even if he were given a transfusion right now, his organs had been damaged by the loss of oxygen. His brain cells were dying.

Fact: I could prevent his death. Well, not prevent it, exactly. I could make it reversible. If I allowed him to drink of the blood I'd taken from him, now that my body had changed its cellular structure, he would die in his normal time, and then re-awaken.

Fact: He had asked me to reverse his death.

According to all the lofty principles I claimed to live by, his life was his. If he wanted to keep it, I had no right to take it. Yes, he had already deeded it to me. We had a contract, as it were. But was that binding? Could he give me his life?

Dammit, I wasn't sure; and he was now saying it wasn't up to me. He was attempting to claim his life back – now, when he'd reached the very limit of his endurance, and was going to die, certainly.

Little brat! I could have killed him for putting me through this bout of indecision!

But that was the problem. Could I really?

What about others who might be affected, if I gave him what he wanted? What about those he'd kill as a vampire? Did I have the right...?

I dismissed that line of thought. Certainly I had the right. I could make him a vampire, but only he could decide how he'd use his vampirism.

Conversely, was I responsible for saving his life, once he had made the decision which would, ultimately, end it if I did not intervene? Another interesting moral question. I could easily argue either side of it. Yes, I was responsible, because I had agreed to be part of his suicide. I was old – very old – and had the experience to know that many suicides – even successful ones – are regretted once the action begins. Or... No, I was not responsible. He had made a request, the wisdom of which I'd openly questioned. He had badgered me until I'd done what he wanted... and then he'd changed his mind. Since the contract was broken, I owed him nothing.

Didn't basic human decency require that I save his life?

Well... I'm not human.

But that's a cheap out, isn't it? What are the moral boundaries of charity? What do I, a sovereign individual, owe another individual, sovereign or otherwise, solely because he is my fellow creature, and he has a need I can fill?

I know what Ayn Rand would say. That's not an attempt to indicate I keep up with literature, by the way. I know what the author of *The Fountainhead* would say, because she once answered that question for me. I met her in California, during the early years of her life. She was working as a screenwriter and extra in Hollywood. I have always been enamored of new technology, so I was looking into starting up a small film production company. These were the pioneering days of the industry, when greats like DeMille were just getting started.

I met this young Russian immigrant on the set of *The King of Kings* (the one with H.B. Warner as Jesus – not Jeffrey Hunter.) She fascinated me immediately. She was outspoken. Analytical. Critical of the way people thought, or – mostly! – didn't. I invited her for coffee. Not as a vampire stalking a potential meal, but as one intellect, hungry to encounter another. And don't think that's a cover story. Of the two, I'd more readily admit to being a vampire than an intellectual. Vampires aren't nearly as widely despised, nor in nearly as much danger. Little tin-pot dictators like some of the Caesars, Hitler and George Dubya Bush don't give one flying fig if there's a vampire in their country, eating their citizens, but true-thinking people scare them. Look at World War I's Sedition Act, or the current so-called "Patriot" Act, or FDR's strong-arm tactics, which caused generations to believe that support for America's part in World War II was unanimous. Look at the nations of the Third World today. Anything they can do to quiet the voices of dissent, they do. I've often wondered if that's so they can hear the voices in their own heads better.

"Your need entitles you to nothing of mine," the former Alissa Rosenbaum said, looking me so levelly in the eye that her head might have been mounted on the yet-to-be-invented steady-cam dolly. "My happiness is my primary responsibility, seeking it my greatest good. It is the same with you. If I could not pay for this coffee – "

"I would, for the privilege of your company," I said gallantly.

She nodded. "A bargain, no doubt." I laughed. "But," she continued, "Would my lack of a nickel entitle me to remove one from your pocket? Or have the army do so?"

"The army would have to take a dime, to justify paying you the nickel," I observed. And she laughed.

Then she said, seriously, "All you owe your fellow man is the courtesy to leave what is his alone. If you live for your own happiness, it is very possible that he will benefit anyway. But he has no right to demand benefits."

I'd always agreed with her. I could, if I so desired, use what was mine to help another who was in need; but need did not give him the right to make demands on me.

There. That was an answer, right?

Or was I kidding myself? Did the philosophy behind my eventual decision matter? Or was I really waiting to find out why he had allegedly changed his mind? Or even why he had wanted to die in the first place?

I had to admit, none of my business though it was, those answers were a factor. My decision depended on them.

I knelt next to the shivering creature on the extra bed in my hotel room. I brought my face close to his ear and asked, "Why? Why do you want to be... this?"

"Because," he stammered, "I d-don't w-want to d-die."

I shook my head. "Not good enough. Becoming a vampire to avoid death is like getting married to avoid deportation. You trade an uncertain fate for a tyrannical master. Tell me – "

I paused. He looked at me, expectantly. He knew there wasn't much time left for me to make up my mind.

" – Did you want to die?"

He managed to nod.

"And now you don't. What changed your mind?"

He shook his head.

"You can't speak, or you can't explain?"

"I– I jus' don' wanna die. M'scared."

"So... you can't explain your motives... that doesn't speak well for you."

He winced in pain. His body was beginning to show the signs ...

"Come on, man..." he whined.

"Listen to me," I said. "This is very important. Why did you want to die?"

He shuddered, trying to get the words out.

"You must tell me," I said calmly. "I must know."

"B - bastard!"

"Stop wasting time you don't have."

His teeth chattered. His mouth opened once, twice... no sound emitted. Finally, he rasped, " – he died."

"He died? Who died? Ah, the man in the hospital..."

"Y-yeah. Same accident... I was in."

"I know that. You told me – wait – is it guilt that made you think you wanted to die?"

He nodded faintly.

"Did you cause the accident?"

"No," he said quietly. "M-my father's – "

"Your father caused the accident?"

"No. I - it was his ... his SUV. I was... dri – dri – "

"I see. You were driving your father's SUV. And."

Pain shone in his eyes. They welled with tears. "And I lived!" he spat. "That guy's car hit mine, and I lived!"

I stopped. I had to consider, not just his words, but the emotion behind them. He uttered the words "I lived," as though they were an accusation. A confession of heinous crime. A self-damnation.

"Don't you g-get it?" he rasped. "Don't you watch the news? SUV's kill people."

"The news," I said faintly... As I've said, I avoided mainstream news whenever possible. I had heard background noise from the humans about sport utility vehicles, though. "They.. roll over," I muttered.

"That's not the point," he said, as though speaking to an idiot. "The point is... that drivers in SUVs... are more likely to survive an accident."

"So you believe that... that the other driver would have lived... if you'd been in a Honda Civic?"

He shook his head. "No. But I ... prob'ly woulda... died."

"... because... the SUV is... safer?"

He nodded.

"So... you benefitted from the design of the vehicle... and lived."

He nodded again. "Not fair. Not right for some people to be safer than others. I should have died... like that guy."

* * *

I am in the supermarket, faced with another moral quandary.

I don't often enter supermarkets. As you might guess, I have little use for human food. Recently, though, I've taken in a cat, and he has material needs. Litter. Food.

Humans are impractical. That's why I like the cat. He's an honest predator. Brings me mice occasionally. A good cat owner knows this is a tribute to him. It should be met with praise and affection, in the spirit in which it is given.

Okay, perhaps not all pet owners can bring themselves to really show their appreciation, as I do, and consume part of the tribute. My cat certainly seemed pleased the first time that I drank the blood of his live catch, and gave him the rest to eat.

As he brings me gifts, I try to repay in kind. He likes milk. There's some chatter in the media now about most cats being lactose intolerant. My experience, however, is that they love milk. I doubt nature would make them allergic to something they crave. So today, I've decided to buy him a carton of milk. And there, on the back, is my quandary: a smiling face, beneath the words, "Have you seen me?"

The kid from the SUV. Missing now for four months. Last seen sitting in the ER at a San Diego hospital. Height: 5'7", weight: 135 pounds, identifying marks... If seen, call the Center for Missing and Exploited Children...

I had a brief, mad impulse to call. "Yes, the boy in this announcement is neither missing nor exploited. His body is in the San Diego harbor, where the portion I did not use has no doubt fed many beautiful and useful fish. So he is not missing. He has not been exploited by me, as he offered himself, originally, as food.

"He has, perhaps, been exploited by his teachers and community leaders, as a pawn of their hysterical attempts to amuse themselves and give their lives meaning. Certainly he has been exploited by petty

moralists who short-circuited his instinct for self-preservation and replaced it with an irrational survivor's guilt and a blind need to make life 'fair.' This substitution made him so dependent on the approval of others that he felt he should die rather than have a survival advantage over another human being. It made him unfit to be a member of the species that's – almost – at the top of the food chain. It made him fair game for all the moral predators the human race is capable of producing. You see, he was food long before I found him. What was I to do but eat him?

"Still, I think there are children who can be helped by your service, so stop wasting milk cartons on this poor fool.

"Hello?"

I would not do it, of course. I had gone to great lengths to prevent his disappearance being traced to me. It would be foolish to blow all that, simply to purge one erroneous record from a human-maintained database.

But I am left with my quandary... is it morally wrong or counterproductive to keep around oneself monuments to the waste and stupidity one has encountered? Would it hinder my personal growth to be reminded of him, each time I fed my cat for the next ten days?

Or should I buy the plastic jug of milk?

WHY VAMPIRES?

– Some Afterthoughts by Steven Howell Wilson –

Seriously, why do we read, write, watch, and tell so many stories about vampires? Publicist types would tell you that it's because *Twilight* captured the minds (and they try not to chuckle when they refer to members of their flock possessing minds) of readers and viewers, beginning in 2005. They would also tell you that vampires are now passé, because *Twilight's* readers grew up (assuming members of their flock can mature) or at least got bored. Indeed, publicist types would tell you that the entire horror genre is on life-support (or is that death-support?) and destined for a grave from which it will be incapable of clawing its way back up through the soil in order to torment the living.

But I'm an Appalachian boy, born and bred. My Ma told me ghost stories from the time I was old enough to be left alone with her overnight. I had to be left alone with her in order to hear them. My parents disapproved of me hearing ghost stories. But,

sleepless nights or no, I wouldn't have given up Ma's tales of Raw Head and Bloody Bones; or the ghost of little Garrett, who died of a wasting illness, standing shrunken and wrinkled over her bed; and certainly not her story of her own Granny, whose voice rang through the little house in the woods every Sunday evening, after she had died on a Saturday night, far from home. She had promised to return, after all.

Because of that upbringing, and my own early realization that Ma was initiating me into an ages-old fraternity, I would argue that horror has always been with us and always will be, because humanity needs to challenge its fears by taking them out, fiddling with them, seeing where their lines and creases are, and looking for factory markers. Is it the real thing, or a cheap knockoff? Ironically, when I was growing up, "Made in Japan" was considered, by Americans, to be a mark of inferior quality. Not so in the horror genre. Some of the best works come from Japanese artists and authors.

But why are stories of an undead creature, who can maintain his un-life only by drinking the blood of living humans, so attractive? And why would I bother to write another one, when *Twilight*? There have been scholarly treatises in answer to the first question. I'm not a big fan of scholarly treatises. I prefer to answer the second, drawing, as only I can, from my own education and experience.

And I don't think it's as simple as confronting fears, when it comes to being drawn to tales of vampires. I think it's got more to do with what we fear about ourselves than it has to do with what we fear in the woods, or in the basement, or in that shadowy

place behind the dumpster at the 7-11. (Seriously, does it get more sinister than the 7-11?) I think it's because we fear that we might just be the vampires.

There it is: Are we all bloodsuckers?

To be born is to need. An infant human cannot survive on its own. Even a superb specimen like Tarzan needed Kala the great ape to mother him until he grew strong. What other creature in the animal kingdom comes into the world less equipped to fend for itself? We cannot walk. We cannot communicate, except by making a godawful noise that the rest of our species cannot understand. We can't feed ourselves, except perhaps to grab the nearest thing and stick it in our mouths, and for all we know, that thing is poisonous or sharp enough to tear out our insides or just plain nasty. We don't instinctually know what nourishment is. We don't even know the rules to Monopoly. If Apple or Microsoft released the human machine into retail markets, they'd be laughed out of business.

Even in utero, we grow an umbilical cord, and a godawful ugly mass called a placenta, which we use to suck nutrients out of our mother's body. If there aren't enough nutrients in her body to sustain us both, we take more than our share. We give her diabetes and high blood pressure. We spike her cortisol levels. We are squatters. The bad tenants from hell. An AirBNB nightmare.

Some of us are brought into being via this beastly process at the behest of our parents. Some are accidents or surprises. Some of us are made to pay for the rest of our lives for the privilege of having spent 280 rent-free days in our mother's womb, or of sharing our parents' DNA. But, for all of us, there is

one constant: We are born in need, and we are alone incapable of allaying that need for a good chunk of years. We have been made beholden to another, or others, and given no say in the matter. We have been entered into a contract against our will.

Pretty mean trick, isn't it?

And here's the really scary part: our basic personalities, we're told, are formed by the time we're three years old. Long before we are capable of going out and getting a solid job on Wall Street, on a football field, in a factory, or at Taco Bell, there are broad swaths of our personality coloring books already filled in with a graceless hand. In other words, before we can learn to be independent, we have been programmed to take from others.

Is it possible that we've all been taught to be moochers? That's a really scary thought to someone like me, who steadfastly believes the lyric from Elton John's *Lion King* soundtrack, "You should never take more than you give." Indeed, I prefer to guard against that level of taking by being damned sure that I always give more than I take, against those times that I inadvertently slip and leave dishes in the sink for someone else to wash.

I'm an individualist. I want to stand on my own. When I need the help of others, I want to be able to compensate them for fulfilling my need. I want to receive all that I receive on the basis of merit. Merit is my standard.

Need as a standard is anathema to an individualist. Someone who wants to be judged by the content of his character, by her works, and not by the color of his skin, her nationality, or their sexual attraction to one gender or another, is generally someone who believes

that reward is earned, not given away like the crown on *Queen for a Day*. (That's a very old reference, I know. There used to be a game show where contestants tried to give the saddest personal account. The winner was the one who came off as the most pathetic. For a more modern example, I refer you to the brownie game in Richard Curtis's *Notting Hill*.)

But a vampire needs. He can't help it. Just like you or I need to eat a certain number of calories every day, he needs a certain number of liters of blood every day. But where we have the option of eating things that don't wear shoes, watch PBS and collect *My Little Pony* memorabilia—and, in the case of the vegetarians and vegan among us, things that don't have a face—he has to take the literal life's blood of a sentient being in order to stay alive. In some incarnations, he can cheat for a short time and drink from pigs and cows. Ultimately, though, he's gotta have a human's blood.

I ask you, how in the hell do you pay a human being for his blood, when you're draining it in quantities sufficient to end his life? And, folklore tells us, said human becomes your slave if you leave him alive?

You don't. And that, for me, is why vampires are scary. There is no way for them to be good guys. They have to hurt people. Maybe that aspect of their character assuages our own need to relieve our guilt? "I was created to be a creature of need, but I'm not as bad as this guy! Look here! This guy drinks people's blood! I don't drink people's blood! This guy enslaves people! I don't enslave people! Okay, some people enslave people, but not by drinking their blood, so... yeah. Look at this guy!"

Images of the Vampire

And, indeed, look at this guy. Look at the vampires of literature and film. They portray need, and they began by portraying it as making us into creatures almost alien in nature—horrific creatures, ugly and set apart, who nonetheless have a certain mastery about them.

Although vampires have folkloric roots extending as far back as the dawn of human civilization—undead creatures drinking blood are pictured on pottery shards left behind by the people of ancient Mesopotamia—the first exposure of a mass audience to vampire lore was probably Bram Stoker's novel *Dracula*, published in 1897. Stoker loosely based his quintessential villain on the historic Vlad Tepes, AKA Vlad the Impaler.

In Stoker's novel, many of the characteristics later ascribed to all vampires are established—Dracula casts neither shadow nor reflection, suggesting his appearance before human eyes is merely an optical illusion; he cannot be killed by conventional means; he can shapeshift, teleport, and defy gravity. He also appears at various ages.

Although women are drawn to him once under his power—he has three vampire women living with him, and Lucy Seward and Mina Murray Harker both fall under his influence—he is not described as a particularly physically attractive specimen. He has pointed ears and sharp teeth, with a long, white mustache, "extraordinary pallor," and looks to Jonathan Harker, his young nemesis, like a cruel, old man. He seems to be of superficially noble bearing, however. He speaks excellent English (with an accent) and brags of his descendance from warriors.

Dracula the novel had a first print run of 3,000 copies when published in London and met with mixed reviews. It was, however, translated into 44 languages and has sold millions of copies in its hundred-plus years of existence.

Dracula's debut in mass culture, however, was not under his own name, and was not authorized by Bram Stoker or his publisher. Stoker, in fact, was ten years dead when German film studio Prana Film produced *Nosferatu*, the tale of the vampire Count Orlok, with a screenplay intentionally derived from Stoker's novel, written by the screenwriter of *Der Golem*. Now regarded as a classic of expressionist cinema, the film resulted in a lawsuit being pressed by Stoker's widow. Prana Film declared bankruptcy to avoid payment of damages and never made another film. *Nosferatu* was ordered destroyed by the court hearing the case. Fortunately for students of film history, it's very hard to destroy all copies of a film that's been released to theaters. One print survived, and that sired copy after copy, making *Nosferatu* into a cult classic.

Orlok is not a creator of other vampires, as Dracula was, but it is to this illegitimate offspring of Dracula that vampires owe their modern inability to survive in sunlight. Before Orlok, sunlight merely weakened them. Also, in contrast to Stoker's merely odd description of Dracula, Orlok was so freakish that he did not look altogether human.

But the first Dracula to be seen in a licensed adaptation looked human… if maybe a bit odd. Actually, the well-known Bela Lugosi was the second actor to play Dracula. Raymond Huntley starred in the London production of Hamilton Deane's 1924 play.

Lugosi, in his first English-speaking role, was engaged when a version revised by John L. Balderston came to Broadway in 1927. The Broadway version was an adaptation so enduring that it was first filmed, then revived in 1977 with sets by Edward Gorey and Frank Langella (more about him in a minute) in the title role. Raul Julia took over to complete the Broadway run, and the production toured the country with Martin Landau into the 1980s. Terence Stamp also starred in a revived production in London.

In 1931, Universal Studios brought Dracula to the screen, adapting Dean and Balderston's play, and once again employing Lugosi as the vampire.

Bela Lugosi almost defies description in his most famous role. Lugosi, who must be called a character actor and not a leading man, is not what one would call handsome. Many viewers found his portrayal of the vampire fascinating, however, and even magnetic. Maybe there was some charm in old Bela, but mostly he creeped us out. Dracula is a freak, as much as any of the characters in director Tod Browning's other famous film. Anyone who allowed themselves to come under his influence must certainly have been the victim of some demonic, supernatural power.

Universal never met a sequel it didn't like, and so Dracula went on to appear, or be exploited in, *Son of Dracula, Dracula's Daughter, House of Frankenstein* and *House of Dracula*, in all of which, if he appeared at all, he was played by actors other than Lugosi. Lon Chaney and John Carradine filled in until the notoriously difficult Lugosi returned to the role in Abbott and Costello Meet Frankenstein.

The British production company Hammer Films brought Christopher Lee into the fold as Dracula for a prolonged series of films, beginning with 1958's *Dracula*, later retitled *The Horror of Dracula* and ending with *The Satanic Rites of Dracula*, AKA *Dracula and His Vampire Bride*. After adapting the original novel… to a degree… Hammer brought us everything from period costume dramas with the vampire to the final entry, which stars Joanna Lumley and feels like an extended episode of *The New Avengers*. Lee declined to appear in Hammer's final Dracula film, *The Legend of the Seven Golden Vampires*.

The Hammer Films were stylish, heaving on moody atmosphere and special effects, and largely about thrilling or scaring the audience. The goal was to make vampires believable, if still bizarre and fantastic. There is no toying with in-depth moral analysis here. Dracula is evil. Vampires, once turned, are not God's creatures. They have to be destroyed. No exceptions.

Lee, as Dracula, is impressive. Of course, Lee as anything is impressive. The man could have played Heidi and made viewers fall under his spell. He's also scary as hell, and believable as a creature that is evil incarnate. Still, he's more of a sidestep into a dignified kind of scary bad guy than he is a footstep on the path to *Twilight*'s emo-heartthrob Edward.

Frank Langella, on the other hand, was a Dracula over whom those attracted to men might swoon, and he was marketed as such. Promo shots for both his Broadway play and the inevitable film version picture

him with his loose shirt falling open, revealing a hairy chest. Devotees of 1970s pop culture will perhaps eternally remember him for assuring us that Dracula loved New York... especially in the evenings.

But before Langella drove fans to heights of stylish sexual ecstasy, there was *Dark Shadows* and Barnabas Collins.

Unlike Langella, Jonathan Frid was not classically handsome. Emerging as the vampire in a production initially afraid to even use the "V" word, Frid's Barnabas was as elegant and dignified as Christopher Lee, well-groomed enough to be believably attractive to young women like governess Victoria Winters and waitress-turned-governess Maggie Evans (and later the obsession of the witch, Angelique Bouchard), but with just a touch of Lugosi's creepiness, a truly frightening temper, and an air of pathos besides.

Barnabas was a reluctant vampire. After the hunger-stoked fog of sadism and rage lifted from him (being locked in a coffin for 171 years can make you a bit edgy), we came to know that he hated what he was, wanted nothing more than to be free of his curse, and, most of all, just wanted to be reunited with his lost love, Josette. He wanted to be reunited with her so much that he attempted to gaslight two women into becoming her: Victoria and Maggie—who looked nothing alike— apparently both looked just like Josette. (Maggie won that battle, as Kathryn Leigh Scott, who portrayed her, was later also cast to play Josette herself.)

Evincing his moral dilemma with being a vampire, Barnabas attempted on a few occasions to end his own existence. He never came out and said, "It's a violation of my 18th-Century principals to

take the lives of others to maintain my own," but he did try more than once to end his un-life. His curse (placed by the witch Angelique, when he spurned her affections and tried to kill her) would not allow him the final sleep. He also tried many schemes to lift his curse, including medicinal therapy (performed by Dr. Julia Hoffman—also in love with him) and transference of his spirit to another body.

The attempted transference cure proved that Barnabas really was not a very moral creature, since he attempted to use the head (and brain, if you were wondering) of a living man to complete a new body for himself, the rest having been assembled using parts of corpses, a la Whale's film version of *Frankenstein*. Ironically, the operation was a failure, but it cured the patient. Barnabas was free of the vampire curse, but in his own body, and the cobbled-together body also came to life as the monster Adam. For a few years, Barnabas lived a fairly upstanding life, keeping his family safe from ghosts, elder gods, warlocks and the devil.

Teenage girls, housewives, and probably some boys and husbands, were obsessed with Barnabas Collins in the late 1960s. He was a brooding vampire, a guy you could feel sorry for. He had a certain suavity. But I do think that, despite his lack of a consistent morality, the very fact that he was concerned about the evil he did was part of his attraction. He did not ask for the fate that overtook him. Unlike Dracula, we knew how he was created, and we knew that he hadn't been a very nice guy to Angelique, but he hadn't done anything dire enough to justify her murder of most of his family, nor her condemnation of him to eternal suffering as one of the living dead.

Many viewers, like Barnabas, probably felt that they were trapped in circumstances in which it was impossible to know what was the right thing to do. Through him, again, they could find a kindred spirit, an unwilling bloodsucker who did not want to hurt people, but somehow couldn't help it. And he had such an air of nobility that he made them feel that maybe, since they shared his sorrows, there was something noble about them, too.

Barnabas's story appears to have influenced the next major film version of the Dracula story—1992's *Bram Stoker's Dracula*, directed by Francis Ford Coppola. In this version, we do learn the origins of Vlad the Impaler / Dracula (Gary Oldman), and we learn that his motivating force is the desire to resurrect, or at least save the soul of, his dead wife Elisabeta (Winona Ryder). In 1897, Dracula meets Mina Harker (also Winona Ryder) and he believes he has found his reincarnated wife.

Hilarity ensues.

It might not be quite fair to accuse Coppola's film of borrowing the lost love / reincarnation angle from *Dark Shadows* directly, and that's because *Dark Shadows* creator Dan Curtis borrowed it first. His 1973 *Bram Stoker's Dracula* (which had no more claim to the author's name than the 1992 version, neither being particularly faithful to the novel) introduced the idea that Mina's friend Lucy was the reincarnation of Dracula's dead wife, who also died when he was the human Vlad Tepes.

Coppola's vampire story abandons any pretense of worldly morality, and deals in eternity, afterlife, the fires of hell, the fate of the soul. It's a story told on a

much more cosmic canvas, and the attraction we feel for the characters is more about the romance of star-crossed lovers than it is about the moral quandary of the protagonist. Like all Dracula movies, it's about good and evil, but it's also far more about salvation than any previous Dracula story. In the end, Dracula's and Elisabeta's souls are safe and together.

Anne Rice's bestselling *Vampire Chronicles* series also dealt with souls—at least indirectly. To Rice, vampires were "a metaphor for lost souls," and writing the series was her way of coping with lost faith. Rice's vampires had a unique look—not quite the sparkling of *Twilight* vampires, but, still, most of them were strikingly beautiful. Most of them were also strikingly gay or bisexual, which no doubt attracted interest and raised controversy, the series having begun after the Stonewall Riots, but before the AIDS epidemic and long before marriage equality was established in the U.S.

Despite this pioneering achievement, bringing homoeroticism to the publishing mainstream, Rice's vampires seem to have all the morals of an afternoon soap opera character. Their adventures are over-the-top, melodramatic. The attraction of these vampires for the reading public would seem not to be about what the reader has in common with them, but more about the American fascination with the beautiful, the rich and famous, the outrageous. Their blatant sexuality above all made them overtly attractive. These were vampires in the role of bad-boy celebrity, not monsters who could be us.

I haven't dealt at all with the idea of the submission fantasy, which I believe is most often advanced to explain why vampires capture the imaginations of

audiences. Some of us, secretly or not, long to be drawn in by a hypnotic presence, long to surrender our free will, to be made to do that which we would never do—or is it that which we don't have the guts to do? Perhaps that for which we don't want to shoulder the blame? Like confronting the fear of being a taker and a user, the submission fantasy could be rooted in the desire to be moral, or at least to not have to be responsible for our actions. It could be that we're just tired, at some level, of carrying the burden of our conscience. We want somebody stronger to take the blame, to control our actions, to drink what we have to give, and, again... to need us. Being needed by others might balance the books against how much we need them.

Am I a bloodsucker?

Am I strong enough to resist evil?

Have I been caught in a trap where I must do wrong?

Is my soul safe?

Do I have a soul?

Wouldn't it be cool to be beautiful and evil and get away with it?

Must I shoulder the blame?

These are the questions. Their answer—or an attempt at an answer—comes in the form of the vampire: a monster, a son of Satan, a master, a warrior, a king, an unfortunate son, a sex symbol, a rock star, a soul in torment, an ill-used lover. All potential alter-egos, all playthings for our conscience to work out its angst.

So why a libertarian vampire?

To be born is to be dependent. To have a child is to make someone else dependent. How does a free person, who believes in freedom, overcome that

paradox? Not have children? But you still accepted someone else's charity, because you were born. So do you pay it forward? Thus creating more generations of people who are bound into a contract in which they are not willing participants?

Vampirism turns this question on its head. Instead of just accepting that we needed to temporarily inconvenience (and perhaps endanger) our parents to survive, a vampire must accept that he needs to actually hurt others to survive, and those others may have to die.

These kinds of scenarios are dicey, in moral and ethical terms, for libertarians. And I'm one of those. Libertarian politics are not fashionable in these days of "You've got to choose a side!" but they're my politics. I can't help but believe that all humans are created equal in terms of their basic worth, potential and right to exist; that all humans have the right to life, liberty, and the pursuit of happiness. I also can't help but believe that none of these rights, none of these equalities, entitles one human to use force against another, even in the course of trying to make that other "do the right thing," unless that other is actually hurting someone.

Above all, I believe we have no right to use each other. I believe that my need does not morally dictate your actions, nor does it give me a lien on your property or services.

But being a libertarian, I can't help but be intrigued by the conundrum of a humanity being born into dependency, and then staying dependent. Why should we allow ourselves to exist in that state, when, in fact, we have the potential to be such a powerful creative force in the world, and to make our lives worth so much to ourselves and everyone around us?

And so it occurred to me that, there being nothing more horrific to me than the thought that I might end my life with the books out of balance, having been a burden on society, having taken more than I gave, that I should play with my fears in the form of a very principled young man, a product of 18th Century Enlightenment thinking, of the teachings of Jefferson and Locke, who is forced to be one of those predatory takers.

Oh, I guess he could kill himself. But A) then there'd be no story and B) another part of being a libertarian is having a profound sense of the value of life and a profound joy in living it. So, while my vampire or I might occasionally do some things we're not proud of, which might compromise our lofty principles, we know how to forgive ourselves, and we strive to improve. We understand that humans are born in need, but they can evolve toward independence.

And that, perhaps, is the most profound idea to be played with when using vampires as a device for telling a story about liberty—that we, as a race, are evolving toward independence.

Since being ejected from the Garden of Eden (for the non-religious, that's "Since human beings became self-aware and began to develop a code of morality and civil behavior,") we have been doing just that. The Athenian Democracy of the ancient Greeks was a step; the Roman Republic was a step; The Magna Carta, The Bill of Rights, The Thirteenth Amendment, Roe v. Wade, all of these were steps away from tribalism, feudalism, and the dominion of might makes right. And yes, we faltered. Rome fell. Jim Crow happened. The Bill of Rights is constantly under attack, and some idiot is always advocating that the Supreme Court overturn Roe v. Wade.

And Roe v. Wade—a woman's right to decide whether or not to allow her pregnancy to continue, really throws some light on the question of being born in need. Where does the infant's right to life stand against the right of the parent not to be used? And does the fact that every one of our parents brought us to life without our consent affect the balance?

These are the questions that led me to write "Freedom's Blood."

My vampire—the one with no name in the story you just read—is purely about the morality of living, of needing, of taking and giving. He worries over creating obligations and having to fulfill them. He is not a sadist like Lugosi's Dracula, a lover like Barnabas, or a sexual adventurer like Lestat. Indeed, he is asexual. As he says, "Do you have sexual feelings for food? Never mind. I don't wish to know about it if you do."

But he serves my need to work out my angst about my brothers and sisters, my role (or not) as their keeper, and how we all fit into this society we (sometimes begrudgingly) call civil.

I hope he fulfills some need for you as well. At the very least, I hope he made you smile.

Steven Howell Wilson
Elkridge, Maryland
2018

ABOUT THE AUTHOR

Steven Howell Wilson is an author, blogger and podcaster. He created the Mark Time and Parsec Award-winning podcast series The Arbiter Chronicles, as well as authoring Taken Liberty and several other novels and novellas in the Arbiters universe. His other works include the novel Peace Lord of the Red Planet, short stories for Crazy 8 Press's ReDeus series, and contributions to Sequart Press's Star Wars essay collections. He has written for DC Comics and Starlog, and is publisher for Firebringer Press, which offers tales of science fiction, fantasy and the paranormal by Mid-Atlantic authors.

ABOUT THE AUTHOR

A Pennsylvania resident, Phil Giunta graduated from Saint Joseph's University in Philadelphia with a Bachelor of Science in Information Systems back in the days when data was saved by chiseling it into stone. Phil continues to work in the IT industry, but honestly, he would love nothing more than to escape corporate America and open his own bait and tackle shop, or explore outer space in a starship, which might allow him to open a bait and tackle shop on another planet. At least he has a plan, but we digress...

Phil's novels include the paranormal mysteries Testing the Prisoner, By Your Side, and Like Mother, Like Daughters published by Firebringer Press. His short stories appear in such anthologies as A Plague of Shadows from Smart Rhino Publications, Beach Nights from Cat & Mouse Press, the ReDeus mythology series from Crazy 8 Press, and the Middle of Eternity speculative fiction series, which he created and edited for Firebringer Press.

As a member of the Greater Lehigh Valley Writers Group (GLVWG), Phil also penned stories and essays for Write Here, Write Now and The Write Connections, two of the group's annual anthologies.

Visit Phil's website: http://www.philgiunta.com
Facebook: @writerphilgiunta
Twitter: @philgiunta71